Oliver and Signe

by Andrew Fisher

opel
press

Published by Opel Press

39 Grays Lane
Hitchin
Herts
SG5 2HH

The publisher would like
to thank Penguin for
permission to quote
from Web.

ISBN 978-0-9560997-5-4

vamboworld.com

For Cherry Hulls,
Maureen Donnison,
Paul Clement,
and Pete Moore

"The attempt to reduce an apparently chaotic world to order, of a kind, by the conception of balanced forces has gone on since earliest history - and it still goes on. Our minds look for reasons because reason, and balance, give us the illusion of stability - and in the thought of underlying stability there is comfort.   The search for stability is the most constant - and the most fruitless, quest of all."

Words attributed to the character
Camilla Cogent, in the novel Web,
by John Wyndham.

Everybody loves a fairytale ending, don't they? Everybody wants a grounded hero to drive a moderately priced car to a Scottish island and sweep a temporarily befuddled leading lady off her feet and drive her to a new life in her outrageous sports car. Don't they? Everybody knows that they'll live happily ever after, because that's what a fairytale ending is all about.

But. What if the hero is a heroine, is that still a fairytale ending? Can they still live happily ever after if that's the case?

And, what if the new life isn't in a fairytale castle somewhere, but actually a very modest two-up, two-down terraced house near the edge of a large village in Lancashire. Is this still running to plan?

Did anyone mention the heroine's son, either? He's had some kind of cupid role in all of this, so he must be fundamentally allowable in the fairytale scheme of things, even though it almost sounds nearer pantomime by now frankly.

He's been rather grapefruit-like up to now - he looks like he might be sweet, but he's actually quite astringent, and he's very well segmented and held neatly in order. But what if all of the sweeping and neat tidying up of loose ends and fulfilling his life's role before he's even become a teenager has left him a little diffuse, a little flaky, possibly getting a bit greasy too? He started off as a grapefruit, but he's become more of a croissant in the fairytale breakfast. What about that then? Can you even have a fairytale breakfast? Hasn't the timing of his imminent teenagerdom sort of doomed him to failure and a life of tyrannical misery?

What if the heroine wakes up in bed about two weeks later in a lather, totally numb down her left side, making whimpering noises from searing cramp in her calf? She's over the moon that she's sharing her bed, but missing being able to be in the middle of it, rather than pushed on to one side. And the fact that she used to lie in the middle, and that all of this sweeping up has happened at a point in her life where she is not exactly a fairy weight has meant that the two of them regularly roll together and bang heads at four in the morning. What's all that about? And even with a comfortable, and comforting, layer of visceral fat around her, she's quite forgotten how physically bruised and mentally raw you can feel with a new relationship.

Let alone the awfulness, the battleship greyedness of her knicker drawer, that single, soft, beige and beiging, bearable bra, and having to acknowledge its very existence, having to let it be seen. It's so very old, but it's never been seen before, let alone had to have its drawer shared.

Did anyone think that a fairytale ending could turn out like this? Would they still want one if it did?

Part one

"What're you doing?"

"Nothing. What're *you* doing?"

"Nothing. Walking the dog. Where's your dog?"

"My mum won't let me have one."

"That's bad. Can't you get your dad to work on her?"

"Haven't got a dad."

"That's bad. Did he run off?"

"No, never ever had one. I've got Fiona instead."

"You can't have two mums."

"I haven't. I've got Mum, and I've got Fiona."

"Is your mum some kind of lesbian or something then?"

"Well, yes actually. Isn't yours?"

"No."

"Not yet."

"Don't!"

"What kind of dog is that?"

"Basenji."

"What's his name?"

"Askia. Anyway, what *are* you doing?"

"Biology project, timing how long dragonflies take to come out of the water and fly away. Look."

"Eurgh. Looks like a hairy bird poo."

"And look at that one."

"That's worse. That's some kind of tiny monster."

"It looked like the other one thirty minutes ago. Thirty six minutes ago to be precise. You have to wait."

"I can't be doing with that."

"Well go and walk your dog and come back when you've finished."

*

"That's not much of a walk."

"It's not much of a wood."

"That's fair I suppose."

"What's happened?"

"The hairy bird poo has turned into that."

"The monster."

"And the monster has turned into that."

"Heurhe. That's stunning. Look at it move its eyes! It's looking at me!"

"She is. They're very inquisitive, and she's also scared you'll eat her. She'll be flying soon if you can bear to wait another couple of minutes."

"What's it called?"

"The dragonfly? Southern hawker."

"You won't like that."

"Why not?"

"No-one round here likes southerners."

"It's just a name. Anyway, Fiona used to live in the south, and most of the time she sounds like a southerner to me, and she's all right."

"Do you come from round here then even if she don't?"

"I was born here and I've lived here all my life. Where have you come from?"

"Wolverhampton. But I was born in Shropshire. I've lived everywhere I have."

"I don't like the sound of that. What's your name?"

"Signe. What's yours?"

"That's a funny old name, mine's Oliver."

"That's a funny old name too."

"Look, it's beating its wings, it's going to fly."

"The noise of it. There it goes."

"Eleven seventeen. It's a nice day for it."

"Do they really only live for one day?"

"That's already been alive for at least three years in the pond. It'll live for weeks now."

"She's coming back!"

"I told you they were inquisitive. That's why they're my favourite. And she's not scared of you now, because you'll never catch her."

"And it came from that hairy bird poo?"

"It came from this. Hold out your hand."

"That is a monster. It's like brown paper, oh, it's blown away."

"It's just a shell the dragonfly breaks out of."

"I'd better go."

"Okay. See you."

"See you. And you have got a dad, even if he hasn't got you a dog."

"Whatever."

*

"He's not back yet."

"It's only just gone one. You know he never eats what we eat anyway."

"I can't believe how understanding he's been."

"I think he's understood much more than I have for much longer, frankly."

"I don't think I've ever known anyone as

grounded as he is. Still, he's got roots. You're more likely to know who you are if you know where you are."

"I'm sure you'll settle in. You've only been here two weeks."

"You don't look sure."

"Well I've never felt settled here myself."

"But you've been here for fifteen years."

"Fourteen. But I'm not from round here."

"You were born ten miles away."

"Eight. Of course it's easier for you than for me, you're so completely alien there's no point thinking about it."

"You do know you're absolutely barking don't you?"

"I sincerely hope so. Come on, we may as well eat. He won't be long. He'll be embarrassed if he thinks we've waited for him."

*

"Oliver! Are you okay? Sit down. No, don't sit down. Oh, you're soaking. Sit in the kitchen. Stand. What on earth happened?"

"Fell in the pond."

"Oh God I knew that was a stupid idea for a project. But you promised you'd be careful."

"I was careful."

"And how on earth did you get that bruise?"

"What bruise?"

"This one."

"Don't know. Oh I must have hit myself as I fell in."

"On the inside of your arm?"

"Well, yeah, I guess."

"What's been going on? What actually happened."

"Nothing. I told you, I was careful, but I turned round a bit quick and fell in."

"And got the bruise?"

"And got the bruise."

"Take off your clothes and go and have a shower. I'll make you some beans on toast. You must be freezing."

*

"You've been rearranging the dishwasher again haven't you?"

"Slanderous."

"You have, haven't you? You're so controlling."

"I've never encountered such nestling cutlery. I had to manually rewash four knives and countless spoons yesterday."

"I really do have to go and get my car tomorrow you know, it is going to take a while, you are going to be in charge alone. You're not going to start fiddling with the shoes or something whilst I'm away are you?"

"The only thing that shoe cupboard needs is a small fire."

"I'm not going to find all the socks paired and balled again am I?"

"But you said you liked them like that."

"I panicked. Any reasonable person would

have done the same."

"It was all so inefficient everywhere, especially in the kitchen. You agreed: we need the space in the drawers."

"And you also agreed to A: Try and avoid checking all of the food for its sell or use by dates, and, B: If that proved impossible, then at least to stick the items thrown out down on to the shopping list, and preferably before you'd thrown them out. I was in Oliver's room the other day and found a couple of sachets of ketchup salted away in case of another disaster like last Thursday."

"But you hadn't even put it in the fridge!"

"You've really spent far too long in the south."

"At least I don't lecture spiders."

"It's so slack. The kitchen is full of these little flies and they are so annoying. If it would just make a bit more of an effort with its web spinning. And we only got those flies since we brought back that plant from your mum's conservatory. It was mithered in them."

"I may rearrange dishwashers, but at least I don't corral small flies towards dusty cobwebs."

"Do you believe him?"

"What do you mean?"

"Did he fall? Or was he pushed?"

"Oh Mandy, of course I believe him. Look, he's coming back down. Did all of the dragonflies come out okay today Oliver?"

"One didn't. Malformed wings."

"Oh poor thing. What did you do with it?"

"I ought to have squashed it really, but I put it

in a tree so it could look down.   If it falls off then at least it's sort of flown."

"Come on, those beans'll be getting cold."

*

"God, you're right, it's covered in little flies."

"Told you."

"I'll have to chuck it out."

"You can't, it's an authentic memento of of The Scottish Isles.   We'll have to get a spray or something."

"Don't like sprays."

"That doesn't sound much like a scientist talking."

"I don't like sprays in an enclosed environment, it's all right outside where there's no chance of prolonged exposure and accumulation, but not indoors, especially where there are less than fully developed immune systems present."

"Let's not get a spray then."

"I'll have to chuck it out."

"Just bung it in the yard for a while."

"Mmn."

*

"You didn't have to both come on to the platform to see me off.   I'll only be gone until late tomorrow."

"Touchy.   Are you meeting someone on the train?   Got some little assignation set up?"

"I so don't think so.   You did ring your mum

didn't you?   She knows I'm coming?"

"Of course.   You know I'd go and get it for you."

"It's my car."

"Do you not trust me to look after it?"

"No.   It's nothing personal you know, I wouldn't trust anyone, that's all."

"Here comes the train."

"See you soon.   Look after Oliver."

"What about me?"

"See you.   You look after Fiona.   Keep her away from the cupboards."

"I will."

"Don't get bored on the train."

"That's a luxury I want to indulge in actually."

"See you."

"Bye."

"Bye Mum."

*

"Fiona?"

"Yes, Oliver."

"Do you like dogs?"

The train would have been full of commuters heading into Manchester during the week, but this early on a Saturday morning it was blissfully empty. I stretched out my feet and closed my eyes and scanned down my body from the top of my head to the tips of my toes. My head ached, and my eyebrows itched. I could feel my nostrils were clenched slightly and tried to unclench them and failed. I slightly shallowed my breathing and tried again. Better. The train smelled. It smelled sweaty, meaty, it smelled of too many additives in overpriced sugary drinks, it smelled of hot shredded damp paper and soon to be regretted late night food solutions. It smelled of Friday night. I opened my eyes. It didn't look like Friday night, so someone must have cleaned it slightly, but not nearly enough. I closed my eyes again, but I couldn't scan a thing to save my life, so I looked out of the window. The train was already drawing into the first station.

*

"Well Oliver, what do you want to do today?"
    "I've got to go down to the pond."
    "Oh no, not after yesterday."
    "I've only got today and tomorrow to go."
    "Surely you've got enough data."
    "It won't have any meaning unless I complete two weeks' worth."
    "All right. But I'm coming with you."
    "Oh no."
    "Oh yes."

"Oh kay, but just today."

*

"Hello Ms Thompson."

"Oh, hello, Celia isn't it?"

"That's right, how clever of you to remember."

"On a good day I can remember my own name too."

"Where are you going?"

"Mm, Skye, actually."

"Wow, what an adventure."

"Picking up an abandoned car."

"Couldn't you just, well, abandon it?"

"It did cross my mind, and the price of the ticket to go and get it was almost as much as it's worth, but I'm rather attached to it, so I've got to go. Where are you going?"

"Marseille."

"I'd say going to the south of France was romantic, but I'm not so sure about Marseille. That sounds like an Italian holiday in downtown Naples with no daytrips out."

"I'm going to see my mum. She was born there and has lived there all her life."

"Oh no, ground swallow me up. I am sorry. What do I know, I've never been there. I mean I've never been to Bacup either and I've told people that it's the worst place on earth for all of my life."

"My dad comes from Bacup."

"If I club you over the head it's only because I want to erase the last two minutes from your memory. You must completely hate my guts."

"No. I've always thought you were just straight and funny."

"I'm not so sure about any of that really. Where are you studying? I saw you passed well. Or have you graduated? Time seems to pass so quickly."

"Marseille, as I said."

"Wow, I bet they have great art schools there."

"I'm joking. I've been doing shitty little jobs here, and I'm going there to work in my Mum's café, actually. I never went to university."

"What? But you can't, that's not, you're so talented."

"Ms Thompson?"

"What?"

"Can I ask you a personal question?"

"Yes. I might not answer it though, depends what it is."

"Did you get a grant to go to university?"

"Oh yes, I was the very last year with a full maintenance grant, loans came in the year after."

"And did you have to pay tuition fees?"

"Lord no. I had a friend who looked at them in the UCCA book. She said she wasn't going to apply to Exeter because the fees were more there. She took all sorts of persuading that they were for foreign students only. Can you imagine?"

"Hgm. And did you spend any time on the dole? And getting housing benefit? When you graduated?"

"Not for long enough, but I did for a while. Ran back home. That felt like an admission of total abject failure.   Took me years to get over it, it did."

"Then I might tentatively suggest that you haven't got a bloody clue about anything in the whole world."

"Oh."

"And I can't see that there's anything a university can teach me about art that I can't learn, better, and faster, and deeper, by working all hours in a rough café in the south of France with that light."

"'With that light'.   Oh God I've never been to Marseille, but I have seen that light."

"I'm sure they have nice light in Skye."

"They do, they really do, but I'm coming back here when I've got the car."

"Oh yes, you said.   Oh."

"Are you coming back?"

"I doubt it."

"Can you speak French?"

"I spent the first five years of my life there.   I had to be dragged screaming into the car to come here.   I didn't talk to anyone at school for two years, and refused to learn English for ages afterwards."

"Well you speak it pretty well now.   Could we start again please, without me being an arse at the beginning this time?"

"Okay."

"Well you've packed light, I'm taking more with me for one night away.   I'm very jealous. Where's your portfolio?"

"I've been staying in a box room in a shared

house with a yard. I burned everything in the yard yesterday. Except for my two sculptures. Those I hammered to pieces in a hessian sack."

"Oh eurgh. But where's your brushes?"

"I've got a couple of pencils. And I'm sure there are old menus I can scrawl on. And I do believe other artistic paraphernalia is available in foreign climes as well as these more civilised places."

"Sarky. What kind of house with a yard?"

"Just a two-up two-down little cottage."

"Rent, or"

"I think I can be quite sure I will never own a house in my whole life. Do you know how much a tiny two-up two-down little cottage costs to buy these days? It's bad enough what they ask you to pay let alone what it finally costs when they've gone to sealed bids and you've got various loans and savings cobbled together with a limited-time mortgage offer up against some person creaming off the profits of their buy-to-let kingdom that can just peel twenty pound notes off an infinite supply and offer twenty grand over the asking price. Never mind paying some cheap lawyer a fortune to badly cut and paste a few documents and send a couple of emails over a period of four months when they could have done it in two hours and then they call themselves Quality Quonveyancing on top of it. Not that I will ever get within a million miles of that, it's just that I've had to listen to a similar story from housemates crushing themselves like sardines into tins to cut down on the amount of rent they're paying to the people they're fighting to buy the cottages with in the first place."

"Ri-ight. Is there nothing here you'll miss?"

"Soup. Tinned soup, packet soup, vegetable soup that lasts for days and you have to throw away because the base of the pan has turned to charcoal."

"Oo uff. I bet it's all fish and healthy food there. I'm not sure I could cope."

"You can have half a baguette with sliced steak and chips greasily crushed if you like. Like an ultimate unhealthy panini."

"With a brown carafe of rough red. Don't. You'll make me want to emigrate."

"You always could."

"I've never really lived away."

"Except at University, where it all changed for you. You never did tell me what happened to you there."

"Did I not? I'm sure it's not much of a tale to tell. I'm sure you'd lived more of a life before you were three than I have all told."

"I can't say I'm not jealous of your generation, you just don't know how easy your lives have been, but I always admired you so much, you seemed so grounded and focussed, so inspired, like you had a light shining inside. I wanted so much to know what had lit it."

"Have you ever been in love Celia?"

"Oh yes, it's just never really worked out so far, you can never approach the ones you fancy, and the ones that approach you you never fancy."

"Yes. Been there."

"There's something Tony Penrose said about a Picasso, when he was tiny: 'None of the ladies have any clothes on, but they all seem very happy.' If only."

"All of that strife, spread over all of that time and all of those continents, coming back to a house looking over the Downs."

"She never had to worry about people not liking her on her Instagram account though, did she?"

"No."

"Coming into Victoria now."

"Look after yourself Celia."

"You too Ms Thompson, it's a long way to drive home."

"Call me Mandy."

"Bit late for that now, isn't it?"

"Spose so. It's never really too late for anything. You ought to go to university, you are talented, I know you can do it."

"It's not as though there's even much of a market for To My Grandson birthday cards, let alone Art."

"You still packed your pencils though, didn't you? Please use them."

"I will."

"Bye, Celia."

"Bye Ms Thompson."

"Hmmn. Let me know how you're doing."

"Maybe."

*

The train to York was much busier, and seemed to be full of nose-blowing children coughing in my face as they ran past. Still, at least I had a seat, even if it wasn't by the window, but it was a relief to get off it and to be finally, properly, heading north, in a comfortable, reserved seat, next to the window, eating a falafel and houmous wrap I'd bought with the latest Woman and Home magazine to accompany me on the large part of the journey.

I started at the back, but I couldn't be interested in the loves and hates of Guy Martin, whoever he was. He looked more of a Fiona type, if Fiona had a type. I felt that the past few weeks had shown up more of our differences than our similarities, but that had been the case with the first flushes of any relationship I'd ever had. I looked back at Guy Martin. Sideboards, motorbiking, he ought to be my type, if I had a type. I didn't have a type. He looked stressed, he had lines on his face. He had canyons on his face. I looked up at the people in the compartment. Everyone in single seats, most of them squinting at phones, looking well off but stressed. I looked out at the far north of England speeding past me, sheep out on the fields, a tiny river, a bus, a kestrel hanging in the sky. Its old name rattled round my brain to the sound of the train rattling over the tracks: wind fucker, wind fucker, wind fucker, wind fucker...

*

I woke with a start and looked around me. Just the same people, sitting in single seats, looking at their phones, looking stressed, still looking well off. I wiped a small amount of dribble from my chin and pulled out my phone.

29/08/2013   01:16PM

Fiona mob2

> You should be about at Edinburgh.
> Oliver and I are just out to look at the
> dragonflies. F x

I felt a fine layer of sweat form on my upper lip, and instinctively glanced around me.

29/08/2013   01:19PM

Fiona mob2

> Please be really really careful, text me
> when you're home.   ILY Mandy.

I put the phone back in my bag and pulled myself upright so that I could tense my shoulder blades against the seat. It creaked, which I found very slightly reassuring. I could smell a perfume in the air, and then heard steps walking towards me. A very well dressed woman walked past me, and took a seat a few rows ahead, facing me.

I tried to imagine a pinprick of light bursting out of her. I failed. I wondered where she lived. She looked like she came from Edinburgh, she looked suave, it looked like she'd spent a long time brushing her hair. She was much more my type than Guy Martin. I looked away to a man in his fifties who needed a shave and at least three stone lost. He needed at least a stone lost on his face. I tried picturing a pinprick of light bursting out of him, but found myself troubled by olfactory hallucinations of sizzling bacon. I drew myself back to the matter in hand, and almost smote my forehead with the realisation of the obvious.

 29/08/2013   01:28PM

 Fiona mob2 ↱

WTF going now??? Oliver always goes in the mornings. ILY Mandy.

Well really. The train was late, and I had less than five minutes to meet my connection. Completely frazzled, I rushed from one platform to another and settled into my seat only seconds before the train to Inverness pulled away.

But as it did so I realised I had not only left Guy Martin and Woman and Home on the other train, I had also left my mobile phone.

*

"She's not replying."

"She's probably sulking. I'm the one who's meant to be a moody teenager here."

"I knew I should have texted her when we went this morning."

"It might have been better not to text her at all. She'll be back tomorrow. It's not a big deal."

"It wasn't a big deal. It looks like it's becoming one now."

"You seemed to like it when we were there."

"Oh God Oliver, I am sorry. I really enjoyed looking at the dragonflies, I just don't want to muck things up between me and your mum, that's all."

"I'm sure she'll be all right. She just festers, you know?"

"I think I do by now. I've known her longer than you you know. I've known her longer than you've been you you know."

"She's never changed your nappy though."

*

The train to Inverness was the longest part of my journey, but the beautiful scenery passed me by. Without my magazine or my phone I had nothing to occupy me and felt all on edge. If I'd had them I'd probably have been fast asleep for the whole journey, but without them I was a tooth-grinding, back-aching, nervous wreck.

I found myself on the verge of panting, and

decided that that was it, I had to sort myself out. I very quietly spoke to myself: "They are all right, you are all right, it will be all right." I glanced up and caught the eye of a man, well I say a man but he looked more like a boy. He looked half disgusted and half fascinated. I felt worse, but I was pleased to note that I didn't feel embarrassed. It was so lucky that I had Oliver and Fiona - however close the Social Services noose was from my head - without them I would surely be on my third cat by now and dangerously diffuse.

I looked at my hands, fronts first. They weren't bad - slightly red but healthy with lines down the fingers from years of cleaning toilets and degreasing recalcitrant pans - but the backs came as a great shock. How had I let myself nibble the nails away like that? A decade absent wart had re-appeared on the side of my thumb at a very low level, the size of the smallest part of a head of broccoli. A quarter of the tip of a matchstick. A grain of Fairtrade demerara sugar. It was tiny. A glimmer of skin protruded from one side and I savagely bit it off. My hands were so lined, so scarred, so zestless, so old. I could have cried at them. I gently gripped a portion of my inner mouth between my right canine teeth for the purposes of reassurance, and sighed.

On the top portion of my left ring finger was a crescent scar from an injury sustained by a slipped screwdriver assembling Oliver's cot. It was a ragged crescent. It was a lovely cot, it never creaked, he slept like a baby on it some of the time, and always looked comfortable being laid down in it. I loved that cot, sold it for a tenner in Friday-Ad all those years ago.

I once read a question in a newspaper - if a caterpillar sustained an injury that caused a scar, would the scar show on the butterfly? It was one of those eternal questions you don't want an answer for. I couldn't believe anyone would ever mistake me for a butterfly, my hands had caterpillar written all over them.

*

"Signe was nice."
"Hmmm."
"Seen her quite a bit, have you?"
"Hmmn."
"I wish Mandy would get in touch."
"Oh yes."

*

I had an hour to spare at Inverness. Luckily there was an operable payphone in the street in front of the station. I say luckily, but I'm not sure who for. That smell, that damp fags and warm hair tonic smell I'd last smelt in the last Millennium, I hadn't missed it one bit and the reminder of it was in no way nostalgic. But it was operable, and with it I spoke to Fiona and her mum and reassured them and was reassured in return and walked back to the station and collapsed on a bench and eschewing food or further stimulus waited for, and was then transported by, a train to the Kyle of

Lochalsh, where Fiona's mum was waiting for me. I don't think I have ever been as relieved as I was then to see a familiar face.

"It's a long way to come for a car."

"It is. It's not even a particularly good car."

"There used to be a cliff we just drove them off when they were no good any more."

"Anyway it's nice to see you."

"Thank you my dear and you too, even if it's hardly a breath since you were last here."

"But they were straitened circumstances. This is a pleasure, even if it's a bit of a grind."

"As I say, it's hardly a breath since you were here, but the circumstances are not much easier, though for different reasons."

"Are you all right Mrs Bailey?"

"I am my dear and you must call me Helen."

"Sorry. It's not Mr Bailey is it?"

"It is."

"Oh dear. I don't want to sound flippant, he hasn't just blown one of his head gaskets on an engine has he?"

"You could almost say that. I've only brought him back from the hospital this afternoon. I did ask, but they wouldn't keep him any longer."

"Oh dear. Nothing, er too, I mean,"

"serious, no. Luckily, perhaps. It's like this you see. There was a bit of a hippy commune on the island a few decades ago, vegetarian, lots of lentils consumed, arts and crafts. Stephen used to speak to them and did some work with them I think. It never interested me enough to find out about it, and of course it all petered out."

"But..."

"But as if often the way with such people, they had lots of assorted children, one of whom has done exceedingly well for himself in all of this fancy modern communication stuff. Or lack of communication stuff, as I tend to see it myself."

"And..."

"And has used some of the obscene money he has been given as a result of his efforts, to buy back the land the old commune was on, and has set up a new commune, for the purposes of technological research."

"Blimey, it's lucky you didn't tell Fiona this when she was here. I'd never have got her away."

"You're right there. I swore Stephen to secrecy when she came. I don't think he could see the reason, but I have a small stock of very potent powders that I keep very dry, and I managed to persuade him to keep quiet."

"I don't really understand. I'd have thought that something like this, where you could keep an eye on her, would have been ideal. I mean I'm really glad you got her to ring me, I can't tell you how happy I am, I"

"I get the gist my dear. No, I had two reasons. The second was something she said to me on the first night she was here, but the first was because what they are doing there is to do with things I don't doubt Fiona would have an interest in, but are things I strongly feel are best left well alone."

"Like what?"

"It's something that Nikola Tesla was looking into near the end of his life. Very low frequency resonance or something, and lots of other related matters. Not that they'd said what they were doing, or that Stephen said it himself until I dragged it out of him last night at the hospital after the accident. But I knew that what they were doing there was wrong. I didn't need to know any details to know that she needed keeping away from it at all costs."

"The accident?"

"Well, you know how Stephen enjoys making things, and they required some very complex machinery and he's probably one of very few people in the country who could make it. Well then the other day he tested it. Not that I knew anything of any of that until I heard his screams."

"Good God, what has he done, is he suffering from radiation sickness or something awful?"

"No. Something burned through and the whole thing fell on to his foot. Broke his big toe in three places. You wouldn't have thought that that was possible, nor the fuss the silly man has made of it, although I'll give it is an extraordinary colour."

"But he's all right now you've brought him home?"

"I wouldn't say that, no, not exactly. He's troubled by my having extricated the reasoning behind it all from him. No, tell a lie, he's strongly troubled about that. And he's also not particularly well equipped to cope with the medication they left him with. Although the hospital quickly realised that they weren't equipped at all to deal with him, even though it was them who handed it out in the first place."

"You're not exactly painting a rosy picture of the house we're about to arrive at you know."

"Och, I'm fairly sure he'll be well out of it when we get back and will only trouble us with the sound of his tonsils playing merry hell with the rear of his mouth."

*

"You know Oliver, I love the dragonflies, really I do, and I know Mandy does too, but you can't go through life expecting all girls, or even boys, in fact I bet sometimes especially boys, to like them."

"No."

"Not that she was glazing over or anything, but it's probably a good thing that tomorrow's the last day of your study, I mean for Signe's sake, perhaps."

"Oh."

"Did she push you in the other day?"

"No, I"

"fell in, I know I know. You know it doesn't matter, we're not trying to be the Spanish Inquisition,"

"The what?"

"You're not going to change the subject that easily buster, and I know nothing about it anyway, well, apart from being a desperately unfunny sketch on a desperately unfunny television programme a very long time ago,"

"Oh yes?"

"Oh no actually, you know that we just ask

these things because we want to help, because we care."

"Can't you just leave me alone Mum?"

*

>Ask me a question!<

"Don't rise to it Mandy. He should be fast asleep."

"He doesn't sound very sleepy to me."

"The darkest hour is always before the dawn. I gave him four of the things, it should be enough to fell a horse."

"How many was he meant to have?"

"I'm sure it said two or three."

>I said: ask me a question! Has nobody any manners in this house?<

"If we just keep our voices down he won't know we're here."

"Are you sure he's not asking you to ask him a question?"

"Yes."

"Did he know I was coming?"

"Yes."

"Oh."

"How's Oliver?"

"Doing really well."

"Looking forward to going back to school?"

"I wouldn't go that far."

"When is he going?"

"Tuesday."

"And yourself?"

"Well, in the normal scheme of things I'd have

been in a week or so ago, but I've gone on the bank, so I'm just going in when it's started near the end of the week."

"That's nice."

>What goes on, chick-a-chick?<

"Yes."

"Another drop or two?"

"Well, I'll have to leave fairly early, but a couple of drops more would be nice."

"Has Fiona sold her outrageous car yet?"

"We thought it might be prudent to wait until I got my old banger home first."

"Aye. They'd never seen anything like it when she came here in it. Caused quite a stir."

"It's caused quite a stir back home too, I can tell you."

>What goes on, I really want to know!"<

"Have you sold many plants in the conservatory?"

"No. There's an infestation of tiny flies I'm having to deal with. I hope yours didn't have it."

"Er, it looked okay when I left."

"If there's any sign of flies chuck it away or you'll never hear the end of them. I am sorry."

"I'm sure it's okay."

>Ask me a question!<

"Are you sure he's, er, safe in there?"

"I've not tied him down, but he's completely immobile I assure you."

"Good. I mean, I hope he's better soon. What were these people called, the commune thing?"

"The Halletts. Malcolm is the child. I say

child, anybody I've seen muddy kicking around a football is a child to me. He must be around your age."

"Did Fiona know him then?"

"Well they went to the same school. I'm not sure Fiona had much time for any of the boys there."

"A woman of taste and discernment."

"I think she thought the whole world except for her father was on about the level with the things you'd find in a pond."

"Oh."

"Until she met you, Mandy, of course."

"Oh."

>Ask me a question!<

"I don't think she even thought I'd ever had an original thought."

"That's nonsense, she's always spoken about you, she never mentioned"

>I said ask me a question!<

"Which is a kind thing to say my dear, but I can't say I particularly believe it."

"But it's true, whenever I asked her about"

>Ask me a question!<

"she never said a word, she just talked about you. I can remember a few times when I"

>Have you no manners at all?<

"really wanted to know. I always wanted to know about parents, I was weird with it. And I asked her about"

>I said ask me a question!<

"ALL RIGHT THEN. Do female kestrels hover when they hunt?"

*

"Shall we just have a takeaway tonight then Oliver?"
"Oh yes please."
"What do you want, fish and chips?"
"Can we have an Indian please?"
"Oh, okay, do you have one you use?"
"Yes, the Bengal Lancer. They've got five stars on Scores on the Doors."
"Okay, what do you want?"
"What do you want?"
"I always order the same: Tandoori chicken and vegetable curry and rice. What do you have?"
"How strange! That's what Mum always wants. She'll never order anything else."
"Oh. What do you have?"
"Lamb Dansak."
"Great, I'll get the phone."

*

I lay on Fiona's old bed looking at the ceiling, trying not to feel stressed. Failing not to feel stressed. There was a large faded poster of Richard Feynman playing the bongos stuck to the wall. Various pieces of paper covered in circuit diagrams and engineering drawings surrounded it. It was not what I'd call a temple of teenage erotica.

I could hear Fiona's parents moving around in their room. I wished I still had my phone so I could send her a text, a plaintive request for reassurance. I could not decide whether telling her about this episode was a good idea. It would be a good idea for my own mental health, but it was hard to see how anyone else would come out of it well if I told Fiona exactly what had happened.

The ceiling was plastered in a succession of swirly circles. I tried counting them as a means of relaxation, but kept on losing count, and couldn't even manage to count the swirls down one short side of the room. It wasn't a large room. It was hopeless.

I switched on the side light, an old small anglepoise that immediately started to smell of burning dust and blinded me leaving great purple spots in front of my eyes for ages afterwards. The room had an overriding smell of varnish at a low level. The doors were a plain wooden finish. Stephen must have re-varnished them fairly recently. I couldn't see them getting someone in to varnish for them. There were some runs, and I tried counting them. Seven. That was better.

There was a bookshelf but I could tell without standing up that it was full of textbooks. I was sure they'd send me to sleep as much as I knew I couldn't face the thought of even lifting one up to attempt to read it. There was a desk with a chair, and the desk had some drawers built into it. I hoped there might be some paper inside one of them, and the means to make a mark on it.

With elaborate care I got out of bed, retrieved my jacket from the hook on the door, and sat on the chair at the desk. It was cold for the end of August, but it was just warm enough to bear.

I scrabbled through the drawers with a mounting sense of disappointment. They were filled with small boxes of tiny electronics items: colourful cylinders and cuboid objects with minute numbers and letters and coloured bands. Circuit boards and tools, wire and more wire, and, just in case it ran out, yet more wire tumbled out all jumbled together. It was not the product of the Fiona I knew or was having difficulty tolerating: she would have had the items strictly sorted and in neat piles, and she would also surely have had at least a pen and some paper.

In the back of the bottom drawer was, finally, the small Rotring Isograph pen I'd bought her for her birthday a frightening number of decades previously. Still in its box. Never used. I gingerly took it out and shook it gently, hearing the suspended 'nib' move in and out in its precise Teutonic manner. A further search failed to locate the bottle of ink, which left me with some relief. I contented myself with taking it fully apart, down to the red plastic band around the base of the point which always reminded me of the skirt of a Dalek. The box still had the tiniest of smells of our flat. I unfurled the bible-paper instruction sheet and read it in all the proffered languages.

After reassembling the pen I returned my jacket to the door and got back in bed, putting the box of the pen on the bedside table. I glanced at it twice, and was asleep within thirty seconds.

*

"Do you want to ask Signe round for lunch Oliver?"

"No way. Anyway, she probably won't be there."

"Wanna bet?"

"No. What are we having for lunch?"

"Usual: roast. Oh, wait a minute, we can't, I've got to go with you."

"Oh please no Fiona, can I go on my own. I won't fall in again, I promise. We can't miss out on Sunday lunch."

"We could have it later, Mandy might be back."

"She won't be back until a lot later, and it's not the same then."

"Okay, but you better be careful."

"I will."

"Take my phone. Ring me when you get there and at twenty minute intervals."

"What?"

"Thirty minute then."

"I'll ring you when I'm there and before I leave."

"Promise?"

"Promise."

"And ask Signe round if you want. Or dare to."

"Hmmm. Bye."

"Bye."

*

"I've found this old phone of Fiona's, take it with you and I'm sure you won't need it."

"Are you sure?"

"Yes. I charged it up last night, it should last you all right."

"Thanks. It's a relief to have one."

"It's a relief to be rid of it, Stephen won't countenance them in the house at all."

"Oh?"

"Interferes with something I really could not be arsed to listen to two sentences about let alone the four hours it seemed he lectured me about it."

"Are you going to be okay? I mean both of you."

"We'll manage."

"I don't know how you stick it."

"He's not normally as bad as this, it's these new people."

"I hope you sort it out."

"The thing is I know that I'm a new person too, I know I've had to cope with the islanders' sideways glances and mumbled words just out of earshot, I know I've got no place to grumble. But they've come in and taken my husband, they've taken something out of him. I can't just let it go."

"They'll probably get bored and go back to London where they belong."

"But that's worse, I say they're new people but that man, that stupid man, he was born here, and the silly people who've followed him think he's some kind of second coming, so he says he's home, and they think it's marvellous, like I did when I first waltzed off the ferry. At least there was a ferry in those days they don't know they've ever been born."

"Um. Well I'd better be off."

"Oh Mandy you must think we're fallen off the edge of the world here. Please be careful driving home it's such a long way to go in a day."

"I will.   It's not exactly possible to break many speed limits in my old thing."

"Ring me when you get back."

"I will.   Take care."

"I will.   I'd be grateful if you didn't go into too much detail about this with Fiona, she frets so."

"Okay, so long as she doesn't ask direct questions, I can't lie."

"Of course not.   And send my love to Oliver."

"I will.   Bye."

"Take care.   Bye."

*

"When will she get home?"

"Not until much later.   Do you want some more potatoes?"

"If I eat one more mouthful I will explode. Two please."

"I think we might need a good sit down after this.   It's such a shame Signe couldn't come. You did ask her didn't you?"

"Course."

"Promise?"

"Oh Fiona I feel so *full*."

*

I really did take it easy driving back.   After I'd crossed the bridge I felt far enough away to stop shaking so much and jumping out of my skin at any sound.   I pulled over into a lay-by and found a CD of the Goldberg Variations to listen to. Somebody talented, sitting at a piano, a long way away, a long time ago, was what I needed to calm me down, and as I curled my way through Scotland, on increasingly usable roads, I felt my spirits slowly lift.

I'd stolen Fiona's pen, which was literally true, but as I was returning it to its rightful owner, it was only going to be stolen for a short while. Its owner was not in a position to give consent for its taking, but given a chance I'm sure would have had no problem. A car overtook me spraying gravel onto my windscreen. I tried to not throw my arms up in front of my face but failed and flailed them around pointlessly.

I've always enjoyed driving alone if I can find a comfortable position, and then sit there, mull over what's happened, what I want to do, swear outrageously at the behaviour of other road users without the possibility of raised eyebrows from the passenger seat, have the car as warm as I like or the window as wound down as I want, sing along to songs, improvise spellbinding bass lines to renaissance minuets, cry at the memory of Oliver's investiture at Beavers, and throw detritus into the passenger footwell without a single care in the world.

But I could not get comfortable, and as the journey lengthened, and seemed never ending, I sat in a jam when I had just managed to pass Glasgow right at the point it should have all started flowing freely, my neck went into some kind of spasm and my foot slipped off the clutch and the car stalled in the slow lane and stopped and somebody drove into the back of me and I seriously thought that it might be preferable if my life ended, right now, in a roadworks traffic jam on the A74, rather than I had to sort out the pitiable mess it had sunk to.

"Are you all right lassie?"

"Yes thanks, my foot slipped off the clutch. Sorry."

"Yer not meant to say sorry you know. Oh look, there's nothing wrong with them anyway, going so slow with the roadworks."

"But look, at your number plate, and what it's on."

"It was always like that. Are you sure you're all right, you look a bit peaky?"

"Nothing a glass of wine and a good night's sleep can't cure. Are you all right?"

"Shall we get back in the queue?"

"Thank you. Thank you very much."

"You get home and drink a glass for me."

"I will."

I rummaged around and put Fiona's CD of L7 on, how it had got in the car was a mystery to me, but its spiky awfulness kept me alert and my eyes on the road, and the roadworks soon passed by and I found myself on the cusp of the Lake District just as my abdomen announced that it was teatime.

The name of Longtown tickled me and I had pulled off in a fairly relaxed state feeling a need for a good break, when I saw a large pot hole on the side of the road, swerved to avoid it, failed, heard a clump and a slight squeak and twenty feet later I knew I had just destroyed the tyre on the passenger side at the front. I rolled the car to a halt and swore loudly.

*

"I'll get it."

"It can't be Mum, she's got no phone."

"Oh hello Mandy, where are you?"

"Oh no, how?"

"Bloody councils, country's going to rack and ruin, whacking over some asphalt with a spade and calling it a job done. Whose phone have you got?"

"That old thing."

"I can't remember. Umm, I'll find it somewhere and send you a text. Have you rung the recovery people?"

"You what? Look, leave it to me. Don't you dare try and change it yourself."

"It's not a judgment on your practical abilities."

"Four."

"See, if you've never done it before it's not a good time to start."

"I don't think you're too old to change a wheel. I think you're too old to change a wheel for the first time."

"Mandy!"

"She's hung up on me."

"She is a practical person you know."

"I know. I *know.*"

"I'm sure she can change a wheel."

"I bet she can, but that doesn't mean she *should.* We're at the age now where we find someone else to do it for us. Which is what I'm going to do, when I've found that old phone's number and sent her a text so she can keep in touch without wearing the battery down too quickly. There it is; why don't you send her a text while I try and find someone in Cumbria who can be bothered to sort out a burst tyre on a Sunday afternoon?"

*

I calmed my breathing down and approached the problem in a realistic manner. I was by the side of a busy road with a fair camber on it and a soft grass verge. It would not be a good idea to change the wheel if someone could do it for me. I would give Fiona fifteen minutes to find someone to do that and get back in touch with me.

Oliver sent me a text and I replied with one indicating my position as well as I could describe it. It was nearly six o'clock. I drank some water and crunched my way into a pellet of chewing gum that was probably two years past its use by date. I could feel it trying to suck my fillings out, so I leaned over and opened the passenger window and threw it out.

"Litter bug."

Fiona's phone made a sound of two wooden blocks, one slightly longer than the other, being struck in succession. It made me smile. The text didn't: Nobody would be able to fix my wheel, but there was a Premier Inn two miles back down the road in which Fiona had reserved a bedroom for me.

I got out of the car and opened the boot. Its carpet was frayed at the edges, and the spare wheel had cracks all down the side of the tyre rubber. I lifted it up, just, it was surprisingly heavy, and it clattered out of the car onto the road. The jack was rusty, and as I put my hand, blackened by the tyre, onto it I saw the blob of brown grease on its side a millisecond too late. I stood at the back of the car looking at the deflated tyre at the front, the nose of the car pointing morosely down, and then threw the jack and wheel back into the boot and wiped my hands on the grass of the verge. I looped my arm through the strap of my bag and started walking back down the road at a very slow pace.

*

Two hours later I lay back against the four pillows I'd arranged at the head of the bed and stretched like a pampered pooch. I couldn't say things had worked out badly: I had eaten, I had showered, and cleaned all of the tyre and grease and rust off my hands. I had the prospect of a lazy evening watching rubbish telly with nobody to please but myself.

Fiona's old phone lay on the bed next to me, charging. What a practical mother-in-some-kind-of-law I had, to send me off not only with the phone but the means to charge it too. As it lay there, it caught more of my attention than Countryfile, and I idly thought about how many of my phone numbers it contained.

...

Lydia M	☎ ✉ 📁 💾
Mal W	☎ ✉ 📁 💾
Mandy H	☎ ✉ 📁 💾
Mandy M	☎ ✉ 📁 💾
Meena W	☎ ✉ 📁 💾
Meena M	☎ ✉ 📁 💾

...

I was very slightly jealous that Fiona had Meena's work phone number, but I could not recall a personal telephone call I'd received at College that had been anything other than difficult to deal with. A torrid memory of driving home at incredible speed to cut a toy milk bottle off the tip of Oliver's finger he'd somehow stuffed it in to floated to the surface. The finger tip had been a very pale green when the bottle finally dropped off. Justin's face had been a slightly brighter shade of the same colour.

At least it hadn't been a life class I'd run out of.

She didn't have Meena's home phone. Ha. My eyes rolled back to Countryfile, and the lids felt heavy with the day.

*

"Mwaggh! Oh, wait!"
"Hello?"
"Hello Mandy, how are you?"
"Oh, I'm okay. No, scrub that, I'm more than

okay. I've nodded off watching Countryfile on a comfy bed propped up with four pillows. I'm sorry I was shirty earlier."

"I was ringing to say sorry if I undermined you."

"I think I underestimated the position and overestimated my abilities. I got grease right up one hand and tyre black all over both of them."

"Hgnhnhn."

"It's not funny."

"I know. No, it is, I did tell you. Are you clean now?"

"Indecently so. Are you both okay?"

"Yes. Oliver's doing the final summary for his biology project."

"He's spent longer on that project than I did revising for my O Levels. All of them."

"The difference is that he's enjoying doing it."

"That's what worries me most."

"How did the journey go?"

"Well, okay until a pot hole ripped a chunk out of a tyre."

"Before then. Did you see anybody interesting on the trains?"

"I don't think so. Did you have a nice lunch?"

"Very nice thank you, what did you have?"

"Steak slice and a bottle of water, crumbs all over the car seat."

"I've told you you need to have a proper break, get out and stretch your legs properly."

"It felt like there was so much further to go."

"How were Mum and Dad?"

"They were fine, hey actually I did see somebody interesting on a train, an old student, going off to live in Marseille thank you very much. Life's easy for some isn't it?"

"Hmm.   What was her name?"

"Celia, how did"

"I can see your face from here, come over all 'wistful'."

"Wistful?"

"Don't complain - I was going to say soppy instead.   Let me describe Celia - medium height, messy bob just above the shoulder, roots need a bit of attention, never wears a skirt, neat tailored jacket.   Pixie boots."

"You're awful, I couldn't accuse anyone of wearing pixie boots."

"I'm awful?"

"Yes."

"And you, my dear, are incorrigible.   It wouldn't surprise me if among all the simpering you got so tongue-tied you insulted half of her family.   Anyway, I've found three potential sources of help for the morning, I was just about to text them."

"Thanks Fiona.   You have put the bin out, the brown bin, haven't you?"

"No."

"But it's so late, you know how Mrs Barrowcliffe purses her lips."

"Oliver took it out.   Didn't even have to ask him."

"Wow, I'll have to have a night out in a Premier Inn more often."

"Don't get used to it."

"Miss you."

"Miss you."

"See you tomorrow."

"See you.   If we're not in we're getting emergency trousers or something for Tuesday."

"Okay. Night."

"Night."

*

"Have you checked the trousers?"

"Mmmhmm?"

"You've shot up like a weed ever since I've been here.   I'll bet your trousers look like anyone else's shorts."

"Mmmmghmmm."

"Come on, let's have a day out in Manchester, you can show me all the places you go to."

"No. Please."

"Mandy will take all day to sort out her tyre and come home, and you're going back to school tomorrow."

"I need to finish my biology."

"You should have finished that in July. You should have never started it.   Anyway, I'll have to sell my car now Mandy's bringing hers back.   One last burn up?"

"Er kay."

"I'll leave her a note.   Now brush those teeth."

*

I tried to remember the last time I was so bored. I was sitting in the offices of a tyre company, flicking through back copies of Performance Car, and Car, and Auto Weekly. The pulsing bass of something very unhealthy pounded out of loudspeakers at every angle.

*

At long last I drew into the edge of the town. The town was still there. At long last I drew into our road. The road was still there. The house was still there. Fiona's car wasn't - they must have gone out for emergency trousers. He'd shot up like a weed since we'd rescued Fiona. I steadied myself to pull into the drive, but the brown bin was in the way. They must have gone before the bin men had come, fair enough. I very wearily pulled myself out of the car.

*

"What do you mean, they didn't take it?"
    "The patronising label says the bin was full of soil. What soil?"
    "What? Well, I put Mum's plant out."
    "Not with the pot?"
    "No, of course not with the pot."
    "But with the soil?"
    "With the soil."
    "Oh my God, we might as well move right now."

Part two

"Do you want some more custard?"

"Yes please. Did you have to ask?"

"No. Clifford, we have to talk."

"About custard?"

"No. About Mandy."

"She seems all right. Blooming, I'd go as far"

"And Fiona."

"She seems all right too. Not as blooming perhaps. It'll pass. It always does."

"No. You know what I mean - Mandy AND Fiona."

"What about it? It's a different world now. Lots of things worse, lots of things better. They can just freeze warts off these days you know."

"And that's it? The world's better now? You're not bothered?"

"No, I'm not. Are you?"

"Well, no. Of course not. No."

"Hmm. It strikes me she's happier now than she's been for a very long time, so no, I'm not bothered. I wasn't particularly surprised either. Were you?"

"No. Yes. I don't know."

"It's taken her a long time, I just hope we haven't made it hard for her. Still, she threw us a queer pitch with Oliver, I didn't see him coming bless his heart."

"She never once told us who the father is."

"Not that you didn't try to beat it out of her the poor girl. Makes you wonder really."

"Wonder what?"

"If there was a father, I mean, in the physical sense."

"What on earth are you talking about?"

"Could have been a turkey baster job."

"Clifford Thompson go and wash out your mouth!"

"Not that I'd be bothered about that either. That lad's been the making of her, and he dotes on Fiona."

"And the other way round."

"Aye. They're happy, and that's all that counts in this world. I don't know how they're going to fit all of the life that the three of them have in to that tiny little house, but it doesn't matter, they're going to be all right, and it doesn't bother me, and it shouldn't bother you. It's none of our business."

"But what worries me is that it's not just us that it's about. It's others too."

"And it's none of their business neither."

"But you know how people talk. I wish she'd stayed in the town here and not moved out to that snobby little village."

"It's not snobby."

"You can say that, but whether it is or not, it's still a village, and full of fancy newcomers. I wish they'd move, somewhere like Manchester where there's more, where there's more, where that kind of thing goes on easier."

"Yes well, those fancy newcomers are mostly from Manchester, so if people there are that sophisticated, there won't be a problem, will there?"

"Well I only hope you're right."

"Custard's getting a right skin on."

"You are allowed to talk to me at school you know."

"Easy for you to say."

"Don't you want to be seen with a girl then?"

"Well, that might look a bit gay."

"Honestly."

"Are you not making many friends then?"

"Not much. I've reached a point where I can't be bothered, we might move again soon."

"You still have to have friends."

"You don't seem to have that many."

"I have. Lots."

"Where are they then? I seen you round, never really seen you with anyone."

"What's your dad do that makes you move around like that?"

"Nothing. My *mum*'s a big chief of colleges or something, she's always called into the really bad ones to sort them out, and she sorts them out, and then moves on to the next bad one."

"My mum works in a college."

"Not Beechwoods?"

"Er yes."

"Oh God."

"What's going to happen then?"

"Well, if it's anything like usual, loads of teachers will get the sack, then they'll put this one year of students into rooms and make them do these tests that show these other things, and they'll sack a bunch of them too, and then make most of the others do this kind of boot camp thing so they pass the tests they have to pass so it shows the college has improved an enormous amount, and the inspectors come round and say how marvellous it is, she goes on the local telly, and then we move again."

"Oh. What happens to the college when she moves? When you move?"

"Well, I never hear about that, so a couple of colleges ago I started looking into it, and the answer seems to be that the students who come after the boot camp year had no time spent on them at all, so they do really badly, even worse than ever before, and because most of the teachers have been sacked everyone else gets even more stressed than they were, and half go on sick leave and the others walk away, and sometimes it just closes down, but other times it merges with another one and they both close down."

"Oh. And you never stay anywhere long enough to make friends."

"Well, I'm used to that by now. I'm sure it'll be different this time, I'm sure your mum'll be okay."

"You're just saying that aren't you?"

"Yeah. What grade did you get for your dragonfly project?"

"7C."

"Wow that's great, well done."

"Thanks."

"That Fiona was nice. Have you had her all your life?"

"No, two weeks or so actually."

"Two weeks? It seemed like you'd known her

forever. If I'd only had a new dad for two weeks I wouldn't even roll my eyes at him, I wouldn't let him think he had ever even existed."

"Well, she's been with us for two weeks, but she's known my mum for ages, ages before I was born even."

"I don't know how you stand it."

"It was just me and Mum for ages, but it wasn't right, I knew it wasn't right. We're a proper family now."

"So you just waved your magic wand and Fiona appeared then?"

"No. Well, not quite like that."

"Have you never even met your real dad?"

"Nothing near. She got drunk once and told me his name was Shawn, but it wasn't worth it, she was grey for days after."

"What do your friends think?"

"Oh, they're all right about it, look I'd better go, see you later."

"See you."

*

"It was really good you losing that phone. I love shopping for phones."

"There was nowt wrong with that phone, I really liked it."

"It was ancient, almost twentieth century. It was virtually analogue. The trouble I had backing it up."

"I suppose I ought to be grateful you did back it up."

"You should.   And just wait until you see what I've done with the shoe cupboard!"

"Oh no Fiona, you've not ditched my old walking boots have you."

"I've put them in three separate bags in the bottom of the freezer.   The things I do for your health.   Oliver was so sensible, we got rid of six pairs of his old shoes."

"He's never done that for me."

"I bet you've never asked."

"You're getting on well."

"We are.   We always have.   He needed a wee when I first met him and I showed him the toilet. You only get one chance to make a first impression.   And his girlfriend's nice."

"His what?"

"His girlfriend, Signe."

"His what?   When?   His what?"

"I went to the pond with him on Sunday and this girl came up with this weird dog and they obviously knew each other."

"A dog?   A dog?   What kind of dog?"

"Weird dog, tail curled up on its behind like a turd on the pavement it had.   I didn't say that of course.   Made funny noises.   That was a weird dog.   Never seen one like it."

"Okay.   I'm breathing.   I'm visualising the blue sky that will always be there, even though it may feel like a hurricane is on its way."

"Oh calm down Mandy he's virtually thirteen it's not exactly a surprise or some kind of forbidden thing."

"Short or long hair?"

"We are in the twentieth first century you know, it's illegal for a girl to have anything less than improbably long hair until she's long past being a girl in the first place."

"You didn't have her round for Sunday lunch."

"No, he wimped out of asking. I did try."

"But then"

"I'd have had her round for Sunday lunch before you, okay, I'm seeing where this is coming from now."

"No, it's not, it would've been, I mean I don't really mind, I don't want to stop, he can do what he likes, you can what you like, I mean you know I was doing what I wanted I"

"Calm down Mandy. Stop. Stand still. Look me in the eyes. It's all right. I'm glad she didn't come, I just felt I couldn't do something that would appear as if I was discouraging him. As if I was discouraging *her*. I didn't want to stand on your toes, promise. Stop looking away. Do you believe me?"

"I'm not looking away."

"You are. Look back at me. Ignore the people giving you slightly funny looks. It's a large shopping centre in Manchester, you're never going to see any of them again, and they're never going to see you again; they're not expecting two women to be holding hands and looking each other in the eye, but it doesn't matter. Fuck 'em. Yes. Look at me. Fuck 'em all. That's better. They don't count. You do. Oliver does. I do. Signe does eff eff ess. I wouldn't want to tread on your toes. Believe me?"

"Yes. I think."

"Good."

"Dark hair?"

"Dark hair."

"Good."

"Good."

"Good."

"Let's go and get the phone. I think it's time for you to join the modern world and get a contract. You can't keep on paying as you go. It's all got too expensive for that."

"I don't even know what kind of a name Signe is."

"It's Norwegian, or Scandinavian at least."

"You looked it up."

"I looked it up, I didn't have anything better to do and you were away."

"I was having a catastrophic time."

"You had a night in a Premier Inn and someone cooked you breakfast, and some other people fixed your car for you, it's not much of a catastrophe."

"Except my son hooked up with some Norwegian girl as soon as my back was turned."

"It's better than Yorkshire. She sounded southern to me anyway."

"What? Just, what?"

"Oh bloody hell. I bet she was planting Spanish bluebells in the woods and throwing red signal crayfish in the pond. And she had a bit of a burr in her voice so she may have been southern but she didn't sound Southern. Come on Mandy, get a grip, and let's go and get that phone."

"You're right."

"I'm always right."

"You're always right."

"Right.   Now here's a lovely phone shop, let's go in and not come out until we've got a lovely little bag with a lovely little phone in it."

"Okay."

*

"Who's that parked in front of the house?"

"Don't know.   Some tourist."

"Tourist?"

"Well, someone from out of town.   Unless Mrs Hopton has a gentleman caller."

"Where are we going to park?"

"There's usually a space up the hill a bit, down from the bakery."

"It is busy.   What about there?"

"Okay."

"It's a bit over that drive."

"That won't do, you never know who's coming here.   It is the <cannabis house>."

"The what?"

"The, oh hang on let me find another place."

"I can't believe you said that."

"So you did hear."

"I chose to initially disbelieve the information provided by my ears, on a charitable basis.   You are outrageous."

"The curtains never open."

"It could be a Victoria mourning her Albert."

"That bloke probably has several Prince

Alberts, you should see his tattoos."

"That's totally judgemental."

"I am sorry."

"You should be."

"Except that their little shit of a son has caused no end of trouble for Oliver over the years."

"Oh."

"Quite.   They started off best friends too."

*

"It'll almost be a relief to go back to work tomorrow.   If they have any work for me, anyway."

"What's that?   Are you out of work?   What's that?"

"Calm down Oliver, it's just that working bank hours you never really know how much work you're going to get until the term starts."

"Oh."

"Cynthia said it'd probably be twenty-five hours or so, might be thirty, shouldn't be twenty."

"Oh.   Is Cynthia the new boss?"

"Well, she's my new boss, nobody knows that much about the new big boss yet.   External appointment.   That was a smart move, plenty of dead wood in the top management if you ask me."

"So is everyone going to have to leave?"

"They can't sack everyone.   Except me, I'm the easiest person there to sack.   Except they won't, because they know they need me."

"I do hope so."

"Listen chuck, if this new broom thinks she can sweep me out she's got another think coming."

*

"There's a man coming tomorrow to photograph the car for the auction next month at Belvoir Castle."

"Are you sure?"

"It's not exactly practical is it? And I'm not exactly bringing in a great salary, tidying up shoe cupboards and backing up everyone's mobile phones. Besides, the seats are pretty uncomfortable and it does thirteen miles to the gallon."

"There's no hurry. You could go out and get a job."

"I have been looking. They don't grow on trees though."

"It's not just the money you know. You need to get out and do things, interact with people."

"I know. I just don't want to do anything, I really want to use my skills."

"I'm not going to make you work at the Conservative Club. It closed, anyway."

"That's awful. I can't bear this polarisation that goes on, north versus south, right versus left. Everyone is still a human being."

"Working Men's Club closed too."

"Oh."

"Never had a Liberal Club."

"I'm not rising to that one."

"Never had any of them in this fancy village anyway. I miss home sometimes."

"But this is your home."

"Even when I go home it's not like it was at

home, home."

"You're so maudlin. I was thinking of going through my old contacts."

"Feeling lonely?"

"No, to see if I can find a job."

"Oh er. They're not local though are they?"

"Well you don't seem to like it much here."

"But it's my home."

"You drive me nuts sometimes."

*

"How was your day?"

"How was your day?"

"I asked first."

"Usual induction week nonsense. Three troublemakers spotted. One turfed out immediately. Canteen has been revamped. They've stopped serving hot puddings."

"How will you survive?"

"I'll wither away by Christmas I imagine. I almost cancelled my gym membership in protest, and for reasons of balance. Anyway, how was your day? Found a job? Started painting the kitchen splashbacks?"

"Neither. I sent out hundreds of emails though."

"Where's Oliver?"

"In his room, sulking."

"Oh?"

"Not with me, I hope. I don't think so."

"No visible wounds?"

"Not visible, no."

"I'd better have a word."

*

"What's going on?"

"Nothing."

"There's a couple of weeks until you're officially a teenager, you don't have to start early."

"I'm not."

"You don't usually come up here and sulk, that's all."

"I'm not sulking."

"You're sitting on your bed looking at the wall with your lower lip sticking right out."

*

"Hello Mandy."

"Hello Cynthia. You've changed the office a lot."

"I have. Sit down."

"Thank you. How's Paula?"

"Paula's, well, she's great."

"Bad as that?"

"Yes."

"One of those years, is it?"

"Yes."

"Thing is, they're all one of those years."

"I don't think so."

"I do. You always think it can't get any worse, or any more stressful, but then it does."

"Oh I think this is really going to be bad you know. I mean really bad."

"Have you asked me in here to tell me you don't want me?"

"You know you really are incredibly narcissistic?"

"No. I'm also in the very depths of denial."

"Anyway, no I'm not here to say that, I'm actually here to ask you for a favour."

"Oh?"

"Mm. There are fifteen rotten apples in this year."

"I thought we got rid of five last week."

"We got rid of two foetid apples, one mouldy plum and two rancid nectarines."

"Are you so paranoid that you think she's taping this conversation, or have you caught acute hypermetaphoritis?"

"It's all right for you, resigning, having the easiest summer of your life, probably just putting your feet up this last weekend and swanning around with bugger all to do, but I've been chewing my nails down to the quick and sweltering in stress. I've had all summer trying to make sense of the stats from last year, *your* stats from last year, and I've spent this last weekend trying to make some kind of sense of the student body, or rather the student corpse we've been lumbered with."

"I wouldn't say it's been the easiest summer of my life, I've been hither and yon, and as for last weekend"

"I told you you were narcissistic, it's just self self self."

"Whilst poor little students do, or don't, get

through the year, and we do, or don't, get the money to continue trying to get them there."

"Yes. And it looks like we might well not get the money."

"Oh."

"Exactly. You see we managed to offload that rotten fruit last week, but we can't afford to offload any more."

"Oh."

"Quite. You know we had to put ourselves down as a three last year on the SAR, but the way the cards are looking, anything less than a one in the results this year is going to be final curtains."

"Oh."

"So. I can't let those apples go, and I can't let them rot the rest of the barrel."

"Right."

"Keep them away from everyone else, in a nice little room, and make them pass. Please."

"Okay, I'll do my best. And to think I thought you were going to sack me."

"Come next June you might be saying 'Why the hell didn't you sack me?'"

*

"'Ere Thompson. My mum saw your mum snogging her girlfriend in the Trafford Centre."

"No she didn't."

"Did. They were, and effing and blinding and making a right spectacle."

"No they weren't."

"Were. They were virtually having it off with

each other, right there, she said."

"Come here!"

"Calm down little boy, you don't want to be washing yourself in that pond again do you?"

*

"Had any replies to your emails?"

"Hmm?"

"The ones looking for work."

"Oh.   Are you having trouble at the College?"

"What's this?   What trouble?"

"Oh pipe down Oliver it's all right.   Well, I hope so.   I've got to get a bunch of ESNs through, that's all.   Well, sixteen of them.   It should be all right, so long as it is sixteen of them.   I mean it was fifteen this morning and by the end of the afternoon it was sixteen.   It'll probably be twenty tomorrow.   I imagine I'll be on the fags and vodka and raw steak diet by Christmas."

"Alcohol is just empty calories Mum."

*

"You look happier than last time I saw you."

"Do I?   That's good."

"Made some friends?"

"One or two.   How's your mum?"

"Going slightly potty.   How's yours?"

"Don't ask, driving me nuts she is."

"Fiona's car didn't sell at the auction."

"You don't look that bothered."

"I like her car."

"What kind is it?"

"It's red and old and smells of oil."

"I thought you liked it."

"I do."

"I thought boys were meant to be obsessed with cars."

"I thought girls were meant to be obsessed with clothes."

"That is such an insult. Girls are meant to be obsessed with their weight and their looks and being bitchy with each other and their phones and then and only then their clothes. But mainly their hair."

"Hmm I thought they were all just obsessed with boys."

"You don't know much about girls do you Oliver?"

"I know they need less calories every day. And what do you know about boys."

"They smell bad and can't use concealer on their spots."

"Oh."

"Do you want to go to Costa's on Saturday?"

"Okay."

*

"I've got a job."

"That's great, where?"

"Well, I say a job, a freelance contract writing some code for a novel communication hub."

"Hmm, working from home? There's not much room."

"I don't need much."

"Getting paid?"

"I had to offer to write this for nothing to get in."

"Oh Fiona.   Still, it's a start."

"Yes."

"At least working at home doesn't cost anything."

"Well I'll have to buy this software."

"Oh."

"Mandy I'm really sorry.   I'm sure the car will sell soon.   That transporter was so expensive."

"It's okay love."

"I was looking for a job in a coffee shop in the week."

"It's okay."

"I don't want to be some trophy wife."

*

"But this is so boring Miss."

"Please call me Mandy, Sophie.   You're not at school now."

"Yeah, this is way worse.   It's taking so long."

"Well finish it at home."

"No way.   They promised us we'd never get any home work."

"You're not going to succeed in anything if you compartmentalise your life like that."

"What?"

"Phurr.   If you want to do well, you've got to care, just a tiny bit, just for a while, but more than now and here, you've got to care a micro bit all

the time. It's got to be inside."
"You do know you're nuts don't you?"
"Just get that finished. Now."
"Don't bully me Miss."

*

I lay on my back and shredded a chestnut leaf down to its veins. I like fallen chestnut leaves, slender and rich brown and purposeful. Slightly paler brown viewed at an angle. There didn't seem to be any chestnuts on the tree this year. I was slowly rolling down the gentle hill. I didn't care.

Fiona and Oliver were looking around the pond together. They were both rather perky, almost annoyingly so. The sunny start to September had lingered into the second half of the month, and I was using my mac as a mat rather than as a coat. I was absolutely drained, the shock of teaching never failing to floor me, and this year worse than ever, as ever. Fiona had said she'd looked for jobs in coffee shops. I seriously started to calculate whether that might be at all possible for myself. I'd only said I'd do my best. There are limits. Cynthia knew that. She was okay.

I was letting my eyelids droop, safe in the knowledge I'd booked a table at the Red Lion for lunch and that Fiona had offered to drive, bless her. I was having trouble visualising specks of light bursting from the chests of people I disliked, but had no problem with a 250ml glass of Cabernet Sauvignon. It floated in front of me.

A woman and a girl, an oldish looking teenager, and a funny dog, were talking to Fiona and Oliver. The teenager seemed as perky as they were, and the dog was hanging on her every word, alert, brown as a chestnut leaf and just as sharp, just as purposeful. The woman was tall but not willowy, carefully processed showroom hair immaculate, and wearing boots totally inadequate for her environment but compulsory for her assumed social status.

My eyes started to close, and then snapped back open as I realised that the teenager, who looked at least sixteen if not older, and had hair you'd struggle to describe as dark, was Signe, but worse, heaven forfend, the woman with her, presumably her mother, was Paula Nilsson, the scything new Principal of Beechwoods. The dog, at least, did appear to have a neatly deposited turd on the end of its back in place of a tail.

I also realised, too late, as they all turned to face me, that I was a middle aged woman lying on a deep pink mac, with her skirt rolled up showing her greying pants to anyone who wanted to see them, and I was totally unprepared for whatever it was that life had left to throw at me.

Part three

"I told you we didn't have to worry about Mandy and Fiona. About Mandy AND Fiona."

"What do you mean?"

"Do you not remember sitting at this very table two months ago, withholding conjugal custard from me in a most unreasonable manner?"

"Vaguely."

"You remember perfectly well. I think that after their visit here yesterday afternoon you're embarrassed by the memory."

"I'm embarrassed by nothing Clifford Thompson."

"Anyway I don't want any blushes, because I can't say you didn't make me think."

"A change is as good as a rest they say."

"Cheeky!"

"And you thought it was all rosy yesterday then?"

"Of course! Fiona's got a job."

"They've turned that tiny cottage into a sweat shop."

"She's done one thing for free but she's got the promise of payment for the next one and she's off to a conference for these people next week all expenses paid. There are people in their twenties work for nothing for years to move up like that."

"She does seem a bit happier I'll grant you that."

"Oliver's got a girlfriend."

"He's exchanged some words with some southern strumpet when he's at an age he should be making model aeroplanes and aspiring to sniffing glue at a bus stop."

"I'm not going to dignify that with any kind of comment other than it's all nonsense."

"Fiona seems to like her anyway."

"And Mandy's future is secure with a challenge we know'll stimulate her and give her the career fulfilment she always seems to crave although where she gets that from I've never fathomed as it's certainly not from my slothful side of the family."

"Being appointed lion tamer in chief at Chester Zoo does not inspire me with confidence for her."

"Oh come on love cheer up."

"I'll grant you they all seemed chirpier yesterday."

"Good."

"And I didn't get an old-fashioned look in the butcher's in the morning."

"Had you had one before?"

"Yes."

"By."

"That's your trouble, you don't go out, so you don't see what I see. Twitching net curtains, sideways glances from people who should know better, curt nods of heads from people you once considered frie"

"Who?"

"What?"

"Who is nodding heads curtly?"

"I don't want to say. More than one though, and that's nodding heads curtly at best, from people you once did more than share the time of day with."

"But that's terrible."
"It is terrible.   But it's not a surprise."

*

"Can you come and pick me up from the station?"
"You've not broken down too?"
"No.   I've sold the car!"
"Have you now.   That is good news.   Give me five minutes."
"Okay.   I've got another two short contracts and a good chance on some long term stuff too. Things are really looking up.   Bye."
"See you in a minute."

*

From: celia.croft4759@wanadoo.fr
Sent: 16:15   10/25/13
To: mandy.thompson@beechwoods.ac.uk
Subject: It was your suggestion not mine

Dear Ms Thompson

I don't know if you're interested in old students but you did suggest I get in touch with you, and I'm almost in desperate need of communication with someone slightly acquainted with the finer things in life rather than unsolicited male contact of the steak and chips squashed into half a baguette variety.   A surfeit of that quickly palls I can tell you.

Not that I've had much cause to stir an interest in the finer things.   I don't think I've sharpened my pencil once and I couldn't direct you to an art materials shop here even if I had the confidence to say that they had one.

How are things at Beechwoods?   Selling another load of unrealisable dreams to another load of mugs?

Sorry, that sounds a bit too cynical.   I don't really doubt your earnestness.   It just looks a little trite from my box room without a window.

Yours sincerely

Celia Croft

From: mandy.thompson@beechwoods.ac.uk
Sent: 08:19   10/28/13
To: celia.croft4759@wanadoo.fr
Subject: RE: It was your suggestion not mine

Hello Celia

Thank you for your email.   Keep up your spirits.
Think of me having to teach the remedial group of students from hell, and remember I was pulling pints in the Conservative Club for years before I got a break just working as a technician at the College.

Sharpen that pencil and send me the results.   I dare you to.   Just one A4 sheet.

Best wishes

Mandy (my name and I'd be over the moon if you used it)

*

"Not this again Miss!"
  "I've said, half a million times now Sophie, I'm Mandy, not Miss.
  "Yes Miss."

*

"That's half way over the drive."
  "Well, maybe eighteen inches."
  "Whatever, it's an unfriendly act.   It's a very unfriendly act."
  "What do you think Oliver?"
  "Red Lion's roast potatoes aren't half as good as yours Fiona."
  "What about mine."
  "Or yours Mum, suppose."
  "What kind of loyalty have you got."
  "You haven't done a proper Sunday lunch for ages."
  "We've not really had a chance, and then I was trapped in Cumbria, and it's been so hectic since. He's never parked over the drive like that before.

Why can't he park over his own drive if he needs to block someone's passage."

"Let's go inside and get you a cup of tea."

Just past midnight in a sticky corner of a sticky storeroom in a sweaty cafe in Marseilles, a young woman sits on a rickety chair and takes a sip of water from a cracked cup. She pulls a pencil from her pocket and looks at a piece of paper in front of her for four long minutes. Then she sulkily lifts the pencil and starts to draw. The lead of the pencil almost immediately snaps. She stands up, opens a drawer, and lifts a fearsome-looking knife out. With the trace of a smile on her face, she sharpens the pencil with it, wipes the knife on a cloth, returns it to its drawer, and turns back to her drawing.

*

"Morning sleepy head."
"Hello. You're unnervingly perky this morning."
"And you look so sweet when you're asleep."
"Does that mean I look sour when I wake up?"
"Not always. Not today. You look purposeful today."
"I wish I felt purposeful. You look ... brazen, actually."
"Hurgh hurgh."
"Brazen giggle."

*

From: celia.croft4759@wanadoo.fr
Sent: 00:48 11/12/13
To: mandy.thompson@beechwoods.ac.uk

Subject: You asked for it

📎 afterrapidlycirclingtheplaza.pdf [845kb]

Dear Mandy

Okay okay you twisted my arm and this is the result. I've put it in a pdf assuming you're looking at it on a clunky computer because your phone was always the clunkiest one I'd ever seen and only had words and not pictures.

I've shown you mine you show me yours.

C

*

"Now everyone IF these computers will boot up can you all sign in to your accounts and answer some questions for the latest college survey please?"

"What account, Miss?"

"The account we gave you on your first day Sophie. The account I reactivated for you for your first assessment session. The account I rereactivated for you for your first controlled assessment. The account I rerereactivated for you when you had to retake your first controlled assessment. The account that gives you fifty pounds of photocopy credits that you have never used because you've never logged on."

"This is so boring.   We've had to do it loads of times before anyway."

"Oh yes, I forgot.   I first had to reactivate your account at the start of your second week when you did your first survey."

"And what do you think I'm going to say Miss?"

"Sophie, I've reached the point where I don't care.   Whatever you write, it's just a mark, it's just a tiny spike ready to be smoothed out by the others, because nothing you say makes a difference, because nothing anyone says makes any difference, but we have to jump through this hoop whether we like it or not."

"Mandy, can you reactivate me too?"

"Of course Milly, just hang on a tick."

"Do you care what I say either?"

"I care what you *say* Milly, I just don't care what you *write* on this survey.   And that's the difference."

"Do you care what Sophie says?"

"Let's just all get this filled in shall we?"

*

I woke from a dream where I'd been trying to burn lesson plans with an incense stick and couldn't get them to light.   I don't usually mind it when I do stupid things in dreams, but I wasn't happy with the suspension of common sense.   There was a whole rickety old filing cabinet of lesson plans, all of my lesson plans, I was pulling them out at random and going to the back of the bottom drawer and finding the first lesson plans I'd ever written.   Awful rubbish, of course.   I'd been ashamed of them in the dream, stubbing at them with the joss sticks and swearing when they weren't even smouldering.   Why hadn't I just ripped them up?

But now, awake, screwing up my useless eyes that didn't know if they were long or short sighted but whatever they were were never up to reading my bedside clock when I really needed them to be able to, I realised with horror that those lesson plans were okay, that what I did then was far better than what I did now.   It wasn't the old ones I needed to burn, it was the new ones.

*

"Does your mum swear?"

"Not really.   Does yours?"

"All the time."

"Does your mum wash or dry?"

"Derrrr.   Dishwasher."

"Yeah, but if you're away."

"Won't stay anywhere without one."

"Mine makes such a fuss of loading it she might as well wash it all properly and be done with it."

"Mine stuffs it in with lasagne caked on trays and everything."

"Mine kicks up such a fuss but you still get bits of Weetabix stuck on the side of a bowl."

"That is gross."

"Does your mum search your room?"

"What?"

"Like, every week."

"She doesn't does she?   What's she looking for?"

"Drugs and condoms and a diary, I think.   She gets me a diary every Christmas."

"What do you write in it?"

"Nothing.   I once filled in the 'personal details' bit."

"Have you ever stayed up all night at New Year?"

"Not on purpose."

"You're so lucky.   She's kept me up, and taken me out to parties, loads of stuff.   Grownups are so gross at New Year."

"No, she's always a bit funny then, looks at me funny, gets grumpy, goes to bed early, then stomps around all night, comes into my bedroom, asks me if I'm awake, and if I say I am or don't stay still enough she cries and hugs me."

"That's not too different to mine, except the house is full of people and loud music.   Anyway, how many drugs and condoms has she found yet?"

"None of course what are you like?"

"We could go and buy some, hide them well, give her a shock."

"That's so funny.   But you don't use those things do you?"

"No."

"Good.   Where can we get them?"

"Boots."

"You can't buy drugs from Boots can you?"

*

From: mandy.thompson@beechwoods.ac.uk
Sent: 12:32   11/28/13
To: celia.croft4759@wanadoo.fr
Subject: RE: You asked for it
📎 onthetops.pdf [689kb]

Hello Celia

Well done!   That's more like it.   I liked the grittiness of it, especially the hoopoe.   The downcast hoopoe, the embodiment of crestfallen.

I hope you're not too crestfallen.   You've not said how you're getting on.   The college is in its usual state: not daring to look over the precipice.   Such fun.

I'm afraid the attached is Cristal Bic and drawn from memory, but it's where I want to be and I miss it a lot at this time of year.

Keep on going

Mandy

*

"Mandy?"
    "Yes Fiona."
    "Do you like it here?"
    "Where is here?   I like being in bed.   I like this

bed. I can't think of anywhere I'd rather be than here at the moment."

"Not here bed here, but this house, this village."

"I've been here for nearly all of my life, give or take ten miles or so."

"That's not answering my question."

"I've got a contract of work."

"On a short term basis doing something you can do anywhere."

"Why?"

"Alcroft are expanding and are going to be opening a new office."

"Where?"

"Greater Chalfont."

"Oh."

"They want me to head it."

"Oh."

"Don't 'oh' me. Could we move?"

"Oliver loves it here."

"Does he?"

"He'd hate to move."

"Would he?"

"Have you asked him?"

"No, but I'd like to. Can I?"

"But he loves it here."

"Can you put your hand on your heart and say he comes back from school wishing the days lasted longer?"

"No."

"Quite."

"Signe."

"Yes, I know. But apart from that?"

"Parking round here is driving me nuts."

"That's my girl."

*

"Oliver?"

"Yes, Fiona?"

"Do you like it here?"

"No. Not any more."

"Oh. Why?"

"I hate school."

"Oh. Oh."

"Can we move?"

"I might have a new job."

"That's great Fiona. Where?"

"Greater Chalfont."

"Where on earth is that? It sounds like a bowel problem."

"Buckinghamshire, west of London."

"Do they have trees there?"

"Don't know. Maybe. Not sure."

"Sounds great."

"What about Signe?"

"I'm not sure that she's suitable for me."

*

"*Suitable* for him?"

"What he said."

"Oh I don't know Fiona."

"He wanted to know if Greater Chalfont has trees. I do worry about him."

"Bound to be a completely flat wasteland."

"Now don't just assume. It could be high end

urban."

"I have to get these students through."

"From what you've said they're getting through you instead."

"They need me."

"Hmmm."

"And Signe is from round here."

"She's from Shropshire, and you hate the parking round here."

"If I'm honest, I hate Sophie Pallot more than the parking, and I hate the parking a lot. I don't know how much more I can take."

"That's my girl."

*

"This is so boring Miss."

"It's more boring for me listening to you saying it's boring than the work is for you, I'm sure, you know, Sophie."

"You can't say that."

"I just did though didn't I. Now will you please get on. Yes Milly?"

"Thing is, it is boring, Mandy. We never glaze them or anything interesting. When do we do anything interesting?"

"But it is interesting if you'd just apply yourselves a little bit to it. You've got to put a little bit of your soul into everything you do. A tiny bit. These shouldn't just be clay figures, you have to be there, it has to have you in it, you should be running through the fields as you twist the armature. It should have motion, it should have verve, it should have life and soul and spirit. It doesn't need glazing, it should be a small brown piece of clay that is on fire with its own existence."

"She's fucking off on one again, it's so boring it makes me want to scream."

"Well do scream then Sophie, let me hear some passion from you. You've done nothing since September except moan moan moan. Why can't you be positive? If you want to scream then that's great, scream out something but it must be positive."

"Leave off Miss."

"No, I insist. Come on, do something. Get up off that arse and scream."

"Don't want to."

"'Don't want to'. Yeah, that's your problem. You just want to lie there and have it all given to you on a plate, you're so bloody entitled. You don't want to fight for a thing."

"All right, I'll make your stupid clay person."

"Don't want it."

"You can't throw it on the floor!"

"You can't do that Miss!"

"I just did though didn't I? Now scream!"

"You fucking cow!"

*

"Can I have a word Cynthia?"

"Of course Mandy, come in and sit down. What's up?"

"Sophie Pallot just called me a fucking cow at the top of her voice."

"Oh no we can't have that."

"I just wanted to let you know in case anything comes of it."

"We'll have to do a full disciplinary."

"Oh God please no."

"You might not want it, but we can't let them do that."

"She may have been goaded."

"Oh? By whom?"

"Me."

"How?"

"I wanted her to be positive, I asked her to scream."

"That sounds okay up to a point."

"I might have insisted."

"Oh."

"Quite."

"Oh Mandy."

"So can't we just let it lie?"

"No we can't."

*

"Why won't you talk to me?"

"That's not true."

"It is. You've been avoiding me, I saw you turn around and walk the other way when I was coming along the maths corridor yesterday."

"That's not true."

"It is. Stop lying."

"I'm not."

"Are."

"I don't like..."

"What?"
"I don't like…"
"What?"
"I just don't"
"Spit it out."
"I love my mum."
"Oh."
"I can't help it.   I don't like all that talking about how stupid they are.   My mum's not stupid. She's really clever she can plaster a wall and everything."
"Oh."
"I don't want to hide drugs in my room to give her a rise.   It's not me."
"Oh."
"Sorry."
"But"
"I better go."

*

"I really need an answer Fiona."
"I just need a bit more time."
"I need an answer today Fiona."
"Then, okay, yes."
"You're sure?"
"Yes."
"That's great.   Michaela will email the contract over this afternoon."
"Great.   Thanks."
"Thank you.   You won't regret this you know."
"Great."
"Speak soon."

"Bye."

*

"I've said yes."
"You've done what?"
"You heard."
"When do you start?"
"Don't know.   Soon."
"What are we going to do?"
"Well I'll have to move."
"What are we going to do?"
"Do you want to be with me?"
"Of course.   Yes.   Do you want to be with me?"
"Yes.   We'll find a way.   But I had to say yes."
"I know you did.   We'll find a way."

*

"Well, Fiona."
"Well, Mal?"
"Will it do?"
"What a funny place."
"Used to be the stables for the big house, before that became a TB sanatorium and was dynamited in the fifties.   I've seen the film, Pathé news reel."
"It's very secluded."
"Very.   Rather like a retreat in the Himalayan foothills."
"Except a little closer to London and The Known World."
"Quite."

"Quite."

"Have you found somewhere to rest your head yet?"

"Not really. I'm renting a room in a big house owned by an old lady. It's quite nice…"

"…to be away from the domestic clutter."

"I was going to say 'If you like the sound of fifteen grandfather clocks ticking when you can't get to sleep.'"

"Touché. Is the domestic clutter lined up to follow?"

"I think that will take a wee while longer."

"We have all of the time in the world, Fi."

*

From: celia.croft4759@wanadoo.fr
Sent: 23:17   12/02/13
To: mandy.thompson@beechwoods.ac.uk
Subject: And again
📎 laterduringaflamingrivierasunset.pdf [896kb]

Dear Mandy

Not too sure about yours. It's a bit predictable, a bit holding up the third try for the supervisor in a hut somewhere for the summer playscheme and you've put the windmill *and* the house *and* the sun on it. I'm getting used to the hours here and I've finally found a moisturiser that's taken back twenty of the fifty years all of this washing up had put onto the backs of my hands.   Someone offered to pay me fifty euros to pose for him.   I nearly busted my wrist and lost my job that evening, but it would have been worth it the slimey little shit.

It can't be that bad at the College, we were all such wimpy little things!

Celia

*

"Thank you for coming Mrs Pallot.   And bringing Sophie, too, hello Sophie.   This shouldn't take long."

"I hope not Mrs Nott."

"Please call me Cynthia.   Now, you've met Mandy Thompson."

"Yes, at the open evening."

"Good.   Now, this is a formal process, but I want it to feel as informal as possible.   I don't want anyone to feel punished.   I'm not interested in punishment, I'm interested in everyone working together and achieving the best they can."

"From what I hear, there's no working together, it's just 'get on with this boring stuff and shut up your mouths'."

"Quite, but we all have to do things to get anywhere.   Now, this incident happened last week during a three-dimensional study session I believe."

"'Motion in stasis', session two."

"Okay, now Mandy, could you elaborate what happened please?"

"Sophie was displaying reluctance to engage with the lesson. I tried to encourage her in a positive fashion. She remained reluctant and threatened to scream. I encouraged her to scream if it was positive. She demurred. I continued to encourage her, and she did scream, but not in a positive fashion."

"She called you a, 'fucking cow'?"

"Yes."

"I never!"

"What's that piece of paper you're reading from? Why haven't I got that piece of paper?"

"You did Sophie."

"She never. It's not in her nature to swear."

"It's not the words per se, it's the feeling behind them that's at issue."

"Anyway she threw my sculpture on the floor first. That was way provocative."

"What?"

"I didn't."

"She did!"

"I didn't."

"Milly saw."

"Milly who?"

"Milly Shearer, she's right up the teachers' arses but even she wasn't happy."

"Look, you two wait here, Mandy please sit outside a minute, and I'll go and speak to Milly."

*

"Hello."

"Hello."

"It's Milly isn't it?"

"Yes?"

"Can we just have a chat please. Come in this room."

"Okay."

"Now Milly, could you help me please? Miss Thompson and Sophie had a bit of a set-to last week didn't they?"

"They're always at each other."

"Are they?"

"Well, yes. They can't bear each other."

"What does Sophie say about it?"

"She thinks Mandy's got it in for her."

"Oh. Do you?"

"I don't think they get on. Sophie is pretty awful. We just have Mandy though, there's no escape."

"I see. But last week, can you remember what happened."

"They shouted at each other and Sophie called Mandy a rude word and she went all red."

"Who went all red?"

"Both of them actually. Mandy, well it looked like she was biting her lip. Then she turned around and was pretty quiet. It was very quiet. Then Tom laughed, and we just got back on with what we were doing."

"Before the rude word"

"Mandy used a few rude words before Sophie said hers, and she threw Sophie's clay on the floor."

"Did she?"

"Yes."

"I see.   Well, thank you Milly, you've been very helpful."

"She's not in trouble is she?"

"Who?"

"Mandy?"

"I don't know.   And this has been going on for a while?"

"Since the start.   They're just like my stepsisters.   You know, bickery bitchy, all the time."

"I see.   Thank you Milly."

*

"Will you stop avoiding me?"

"Will you stop following me?"

"I'm not following you."

"You are."

"I'm not, you're avoiding me."

"I'm not."

"What have I done?"

"You're following me around.   It's creepy."

"I can't help it, it's not fair."

"Why's it not fair?"

"It's not fair a, because I only said let's hide that because it's the kind of stupid thing boys do and I was trying to impress you but mainly because b, you love your mum, and that's not fair."

"Oh."

"I only said it for a dare."

"Oh."

"I only said it cos I like you."

"Oh."

"Stop saying oh. I'll stop following you, I didn't mean to."

"Oh no."

*

"I hope everyone's all right, that took a little longer than I hoped it would. Now Sophie, I've thought about this, and I've spoken to Milly, and I'm minded to leave things as they are. You were already on a level 2 before you came in, and I think that's about fair enough. I'd like a written undertaking from you to pay more attention in class. Okay?"

"All right."

"It's not all right at all!"

"Why not Mrs Pallot?"

"Because it's a whitewash. You're letting her get away with it. You just care about each other."

"When you came in I said I'm just interested in everyone getting on as best as they can. Nothing has changed with that I can tell you."

"Fat chance."

"Good chance actually. Now, if you'd care to sit in reception and help Sophie write something meaningful about how she's going to buck up her game I'd be grateful. Please leave it with Janice in the office."

"Hmph."

"Nice to see you both. Any further issues don't hesitate to come and see me."

"Hmph."

*

"Well Mandy what the bloody hell am I going to do with you?"

*

From: mandy.thompson@beechwoods.ac.uk
Sent: 23:12   12/10/13
To: celia.croft4759@wanadoo.fr
Subject: thats torn it
📎 ahahyawaemekatotgnimoceryeht.pdf [916kb]

Celia dear

You know you're dead lucky washing pots in the south of france while I'm stuck here coping with a girlfriend who's moving to the south to set up some cockaminny business I don't understand a son who's gone all hole in a corner and now it looks like I'm about to be sacked for throwing a clay man (with a totally outsized penis) onto the floor in front of a student who proceeded to call me a fucking cow.

Grrrrrrrrrrrrrrrrrrrrrrrrrr!

Mandy

*

"Well, Fiona?"

"Well Mal."

"On y va?"

"Oui monsieur."

"Excellent."

"When will the equipment arrive?"

"Next Tuesday."

"London isn't going to know what's hit it."

*

"Well Oliver."

"Yes Mum?"

"How do you feel about moving?"

"Where?"

"You know. Where Fiona's work is."

"Oh, I thought that'd sort of gone away."

"Like Fiona'd 'sort of gone away'?"

"No. No. I just thought. I mean, we'd not sort of said. I mean, I thought. You know, your job, that sort of thing."

"What job?"

"Your job. That one you keep going on about all the time."

"I've resigned."

"You've what?"

"I've resigned."

"But you've worked there forever."

"I cleaned glasses for ages before I worked there. I was alive, I was a human being once, before I worked there."

"You reckon?"

"Aanyway. We're going south okay?"

"No."

"You were begging us to go last week."

"I've changed my mind."

"You're not the proper gender to do that."

"Mum!"

"What?"

"Don't be sexist."

"Oliver, I've resigned. I can be whatever ist I want, and what's more, I shall."

"But Signe..."

"What about Signe? I thought you were right off her?"

"Oh Mum."

"Oh shit."

From: celia.croft4759@wanadoo.fr

Sent: 09:51   12/13/13

To: mandy.thompson@beechwoods.ac.uk

Subject: RE: thats torn it

Dear Mandy

I'm sorry to hear about your problems but I fear that you reap what you sow.

You never taught me regularly but you did teach my friend Isabel. The fact is she said you were a boring teacher.

I hate to write that. You took us for a few classes when someone was sick, and they were great, they were the best classes I ever had, frankly.   But you were just you, you were just talking off the cuff, making it up, cheering us up, keeping us going.   It was great.

Maybe you need a change.   There are only so many clay penises anybody can stand.

I'm thinking of you as I wash those pots.

C

*

"Come in Mandy.   Don't hover."
    "Hmm, yes.   Hello Ms Nilsson."
    "Paula.   And it's Missus, thank you."
    "Oh.   Sorry."
    "No, look, I should have, anyway, whatever, this is the worst part of my job."
    "Is it?   I'd've thought it was the actual sacking bit.   Not the final send off bit, surely that's easy."
    "I'd rather put the black hat on in the courtroom than put the noose around the neck."
    "The bullet in the back of the head in a few weeks' time."
    "Quite.   Still, you had to do it when you were head of department didn't you?   Which did you dislike the most?"
    "The initial notification.   Anyway, I'm not the same, and even though I've done it myself, it's not the same somehow, and I've not done it as much

as you of course."

"Thanks. I am going to take that as a compliment you know."

"I know."

"Ouch."

"You're welcome."

"As you say, you're different."

"Fell on my own sword. No nooses necessary."

"Quite. But we have to speak."

"Another quality box to tick."

"You really don't like me do you?"

"That's a very needy question. The only honest answer is that I don't know you well enough to say one way or the other. I don't like what I think you represent, but I'm not convinced I've got enough knowledge for presenting much of an argument for an opposition to what that is."

"That's quite an open minded statement, even if it isn't an answer."

"I didn't think you were after an answer."

"I wouldn't normally ask, because I wouldn't normally care, but with you, I find that I do."

"If I was honest with myself, I'd take that as a compliment."

"But as you're not honest with yourself?"

"I won't. At least I recognise my delusions."

"Hmm. Where are you going?"

"Buckinghamshire."

"Buckinghamshire?"

"Buckinghamshire. It's almost as hard to say as no nooses needed."

"But why?"

"My partner's got a new job. I want to be with

her."

"It's so far away.   Have you got somewhere to live?"

"I've viewed a few flats online, to rent. They're all incredibly expensive and very grotty. The digs she's in are even grottier."

"Signe never mentioned Buckinghamshire."

"Why would she?"

"Come on Mandy.   She's going to be very upset.   Can't you wait?"

"Until what?   Nature takes its course?   'Your work here is done'?"

"They're quite smitten I think.   Surely you went through that as a teenager?"

"Not really.   I had an awful brace."

"I had the worst acne in the class."

"Poor you.   How have we produced such attractive children?"

"I wouldn't like to speculate.   You know you don't have to go?"

"What?"

"I don't only have to axe people you know.   I can hire them too."

"What?"

"There's always some kind of managerial, quality, assessment, resources, promotion, marketing, role out there."

"What?"

"And if there isn't, I can always make one."

"You mean, for the temporary happiness of your daughter, you'd go out and magic me up a job, just to stop me moving south?"

"Signe means a lot to me."

"Well. I'm staggered, I've got to say."

"But are you tempted?"

"Flattered mainly, which is probably misguided, but I'm always drawn to it."

"Ah well. Anyway I do wish you well."

"I wish I could say the same to you, but I can't. I've got to be honest, I hate your job, I could never do it. Closing things down, making things worse."

"But I don't. Or, at least, I don't want to. I only want to improve things."

"Who's deluded now?"

"Look, I still don't see how things went so badly wrong at Cirencester after I left. That management team was the strongest I'd ever appointed."

"Hmm. I better go. Good luck. Anyway, they've got their phones these days haven't they? They don't care about the real world do they?"

"I wish I knew one thing about what Signe cared about. Well I suppose I do know one thing. Are you going to teach, in Buckinghamshire?"

"I think I could do with a bit of time off that actually. I feel like washing pots for a living. It seems a bit safer, if not kinder."

"Well, good luck."

"I think you need more luck than me. Bye."

"Good bye Mandy."

*

"Please be careful with these boxes, the equipment is very delicate."

"Ooo you are strict."

"Don't Malcolm, I'm just trying to take it

seriously."

"So am I, but I'm struggling. These rooms are so large. I'm used to working in the corner of a cupboard."

"Shall we set the cage up over here?"

"Yes, let's. Have you got the set-up guides?"

"Of course. Box J."

"That's beautifully packed."

"Vermiculite."

"Makes it a bit dusty."

"Just rinse it off."

"'See how a little water clears us of this deed'."

"Malcolm!"

"God, I love magnesium alloys."

"Forged not cast."

"Makes all the difference."

"Come on, let's get it set up."

*

"Oh do be careful with them boxes."

"Who cares?"

"I do Oliver. That's our shared history in there."

"Not very much, is there?"

"Come on love, it's an adventure isn't it?"

*

"Ooh, you've made a new tripole."

"Nothing but the best for your office Fiona."

"God that's huge. What's the kVA?"

"Twenty six."

"No way."

"Oh yes."

"It'll never fit in here."

"Hmm. Let's see. You take the alpha wing."

"Doesn't want to go together."

"It is the first time it's been set up."

"It's going to foul the ceiling."

"Let's get it balanced first."

"Wow, it does fit. That is so elegant."

"Oh ye of little faith."

*

"Well, bye then, I suppose."

"I'm going to miss you."

"It's normally me who moves on and runs away. I'm not used to being the person left behind."

"Maybe your mum will stay there forever now."

"I wish. Well, I don't actually, cos you're going."

"I'm going to miss you."

"I'm going to miss you too. Are the dragonflies still flying?"

"Some of them. Ruddy darters."

"I thought you liked them."

"No, it's a species."

"'Rolls eyes'. You did explain you know. At great length."

"And you, remembered?"

"Yes."

"I'm going to miss you."

"You'd better get going, your mum'll be wondering where you are."

"Don't want to go."

"Take this.   Don't open it till you're in the car on your way."

"What is it?"

"Take it.   Bye Oliver."

"Bye Signe."

"Bye."

"Bye."

*

From: mandy31701@yahoo.com
Sent: 06:31   01/15/14
To: celia.croft4759@wanadoo.fr
Subject: coa

Dear Celia

Thank you for your last email which feels like forever ago and to be frank I can't really remember what it was about.   Anyway I've left the college and we've moved to Buckinghamshire to be with Fiona.   My son is pining for some girl he doesn't even know and he's only thirteen for crying out loud and I imagine I'll be joining you washing pots before too long.
I haven't sent a picture because the only thing I could draw was a tabula rasa because that's what I feel like, but not in a good way.

Mandy

"Well what about this one then?"

"Can you see the price of it?"

"Well they're all like that."

"What are you being paid?"

"You know exactly how much I'm being paid."

"But I haven't got a job."

"You can be the kept woman then.   I've done it."

"For a couple of weeks tops."

"I've still got lots of money from selling the car. We can furnish it really nicely."

"Do we need three bedrooms?"

"Well, if we need some office space, or if you want to paint.   Or."

"Or what?"

"Well, if Signe wanted to stay."

"Oh."

"Quite."

"We could go and have a look I suppose."

"That's my kept woman."

"It's got a nice garden.   Never had a garden before.   Looks a bit wild."

"Oliver will love it."

Part four

"Happy new year Mrs Thompson."

"Happy new year Mr Thompson.   What's brought this on?"

"What's brought what on?"

"You're very chirpy."

"New year, new start."

"We used to wish each other a happy new year at midnight rather than seven o'clock in the morning."

"Daft staying up.   It's only a notional thing anyway."

"I preferred the chirpy you.   What's the new start for?"

"Us.   Everyone."

"Us?   You're not flitting off with some flighty piece."

"No.   And don't say 'pity'."

"I was going to say you'd wear those bunions off trying to catch one."

"I was quite a catch myself in my day I'll have you know."

"I was there, if you remember."

"Seems like yesterday."

"You had nice hair.   But men took so much more care with their hair in those days.   Now it's all shaved off on top and dropped down on their faces in fancy beards."

"Corporation hair wax.   I grew a beard once. Do you remember that?"

"A silly little goatee.   Still itched something horrid."

"I could tell.   You wouldn't come near me. Had to shave it off I did."

"Thank heavens."

"I wonder if Oliver will grow a beard."

"I do hope not, he's such a kind face and a beard always makes a man look like he's got something to hide."

"He has got a kind face, hasn't he? Much as we've seen of it this last twelve month they've moved."

"The trouble is we were spoiled before but we didn't know it."

"Aye."

"I think Mandy's lonely."

"Who wouldn't be down south."

"Get off with your down south. I worry that Fiona is that type who get wedded to their jobs."

"It's never made sense to me."

"I could tell that!"

"Cheeky. Well at least they have Oliver."

"He's pining for that girl with the funny name and the funnier dog."

"I'd better not say what came into my head then."

"No."

"I'm sure he's not. It's been a year, these teenagers are here today and gone tomorrow with their affections. Hormones, they call it. Parking, we called it."

"You never went parking. You had that motorcycle and sidecar combination."

"That will have to remain part of what makes me mysterious."

"The mystery is what attracted me to you."

"I had nice hair, you said. Even then I was just

a sex object to you."

"I think you ought to get up and go and put that kettle on."

*

"Happy new year."

"Smgnnnnnh."

"A charming welcome to 2015. I know you're awake under there."

"Time is it?"

"Time to get up and seize the day, time to get up and seize the year."

"What time did we get to bed?"

"Ten thirty."

"Why do we have to go to bed early on New Year's Eve?"

"You know."

"What? That? You're still bitter about that?"

"I wouldn't say bitter. I'd say, it had an effect."

"Hmm. You could say you're affected."

"That's some cheek missus, it's mainly your fault."

"What, Oliver?"

"No. No. That which made him."

"'That which made him'. You do make me laugh sometimes."

"I hope he's okay. He feels so far away."

"He's about twenty feet away."

"Well he was on the other side of the wall before we moved. I used to wake up as soon as he'd filled his nappy."

"Those were the days."

"Are you all right?"

"Yes. Untimely ripped from the womb of sleep, but otherwise okay."

"You really slept well last night. Your snores were almost as loud as the fireworks."

"Who's cheeky now?"

"Hmm. Are you sure you're all right?"

"I was until you kept on asking me. Have I got spots? Or even worse bags under my eyes?"

"No. Just a temporary far away look."

"Me?"

"You."

"It's almost permanent with you. Are you all right?"

"Yes, mostly. Yes, actually, more. I know Oliver's further away, but he seems happier here."

"He likes the garden."

"Like you told me."

"Like I told you."

"He likes his school."

"Shock horror people down south don't beat someone up for having a funny northern accent."

"I should hope not."

"Shock horror people down south make friends with people and aren't all just money-grabbing sociopaths."

"I should hope so."

"And you?"

"I'm glad I'm not a kept woman any more."

"Not a role you took to like a duck to water, tee bee aitch."

"It almost takes me back to the Conservative Club."

"What, teaching college lecturers? Surely they're all red in tooth and claw?"

"The pastoral side, the neediness, the clinginess, the slightly sliminess of it."

"Still, it's a job."

"It's a job, and Graham is great to work with, in fact, he's a laugh."

"Not another human southerner? When will these wonders cease?"

"He's from Teesside. I'm sure I've said that before."

"You probably have."

"You don't care though do you?"

"No. The 'south isn't so bad' game is too much fun."

"Yer little bugger."

"Don't ruin my day. Don't ruin my year for me, let me carry on. And anyway, it's not like you've shown one iota of interest in who I'm working with."

"Sorry love. You must have them round for tea."

"Oh Mandy."

"Stop laughing!"

"We are so socially inept. It is funny."

*

"Well happy new year Stephen, although I hope next time you go out and get drunk like that you take your teeth out before you get into bed. I don't know who you keep on going out with leading you astray like that. I'm glad it can't be that Malcolm Hallett him having moved away for over a year now. I can tell you're still communicating with him and I wish you'd stop. That kind of person isn't nice. They suck people in and spit them out again when they've had all they want from them and they don't care what happens to them afterwards. I haven't heard from Fiona now for a couple of months in any kind of meaningful fashion and I don't know if that's a good thing or gives concern. If she's just wrapped up with Mandy and Oliver in Greater Chalfont that's fine but you know how she gets bogged down in her scientific endeavours and they aren't real. You've never understood that, but at least with you the things you were obsessed with turned into real items. These days it's all virtual this and online that and people talk themselves into believing that it's as real as real things when it's palpably not. It makes my blood boil with the intangible nature of life these days if Fiona just came and cut a few cubic metres of peat she'd at least be grounded a bit but instead she's got her head in the clouds with this airy-fairy nonsense. I've still not got half of my head around what it is she's doing in this new job of hers. I know you have and I know you won't tell me when you try to persuade me you can't tell me when you want to say that you don't believe I'd understand. It's almost like you don't trust me though why I cannot understand. Do you trust me? Stephen? Stephen! Wake up! Don't be silly. Stephen."

*

"Oh Stephen, no."

*

"Will I have to wear a black tie?"

"No Oliver. I wouldn't want you wearing one at your age and Granny has said she wants it to be a fun occasion anyway."

"Fun?"

"Well I don't think there'll be a bouncy castle, but these days people want funerals to be more a celebration of a life rather than a solemn meditation on the finality of it all."

"Oh. Will he be buried in the ground in front of us?"

"No. He's going to be cremated, and then a few of us will be going to scatter the ashes in the loch."

"Including me?"

"Including you, if you want to. Just squeeze my hand during the day if it's getting to be too much for you."

"I want to see it all. Do we see the burning?"

"No we do not. Where does this ghoulishness come from?"

"That's a shame."

"If it's anything like any cremation I've been to before, there's an awkward, jerky moment with a curtain and a slowly moving coffin."

"Poor Fiona. Poor Granny in Scotland."

"I know. They're both a bit distraught to say the least."

"Will the ashes be hot?"

*

I've not attended many funerals in my life, for which I suppose I ought to be more grateful than I am. It had left me rather unprepared for guiding Oliver through the ordeal, and it felt that rather than have him indicate to me when he wanted to bail out, it should have been the other way around. It felt as if he was carrying me through a new and traumatic experience when I should have been helping him. As we sat there, in the bright but tiny community centre, co-opted as a venue for the seeing off of an obstinate atheist, I mentally counted up the solemn ceremonies that I had been invited to, and realised to my horror that, small as the number of funerals was, it outnumbered the weddings I'd attended by a factor of three to one. No wonder Fiona laughed at the thought of our entertaining her boss, I was so socially stunted it stuck out a mile.

But I looked down at Oliver, taking it all in with a keen interest that had never flagged, and thought very clearly: I don't care. I don't care if I'm socially stunted or people never want to invite me to their meaningless little ceremonies of trite attraction masquerading as lifelong commitment. Here was Oliver, a flawed and vulnerable and yet questing and perfect example of everything that was good and proper in the world. He was helping me through this moment of, this moment of, well, what? I couldn't really say I was grieving, for a man who had purposefully insulted me the last time I saw him and beyond that I didn't know at all. I was upset, but mainly for Fiona, and also her mum. If she'd died instead I'd be grieving, I think. If you've painted somebody you're closer to them than most people know. I'd traced out her outline and filled her in, she was substance to me. But he was a distant builder of engines that drove nothing, a designer of buildings, an architect. How we'd sneered down our noses at architects at university. People who can't draw, people who can't build, pretending they've created something. They were, without exception, the ones I'd come across, arseholes of the first water.

I looked across at Fiona, damp eyed but not crying. Stoic, as ever. Relieved, in a way she could not properly know. She was wearing a purple scarf around her head. It looked rather strange but also somehow magnificent, a bolt of restrained vibrancy, only the colour pulling the look out of the nineteen fifties. It was so nearly early Coronation Street I had to clench my toes together to stop from laughing at the thought, and then a tear rolled down her cheek and I felt awful and put my hand on hers and gave her a slight smile she returned.

As she turned back to the front of the room I saw her cast a glance around it. Her eyes seemed to alight for a split second on a man with a prissy little beard sitting on the back row of rickety chairs. I turned to Mrs Bailey. I had no idea if she'd ever smoked, but her expression clearly showed she was willing to start again, and the thought was giving her a lot of comfort.

We mumbled our way through a desultory reading of Rain, not an especially sensible choice for a funeral song accompanied by an out of tune piano, but better perhaps than It's My Party and I'll Cry If I Want To, which is what I've always wondered about for my own funeral, and which seemed just plain silly at this point.

*

It was with a great sigh of relief that I closed the door on the day. A nicely bland hotel room door. The thought of lying in that old room of Fiona's again was too much to bear. I wondered what thoughts she was entertaining about Richard Feynman at that moment, but she'd probably still be up and talking to her mum. I walked into the bathroom and sluiced cold water onto my face. The fustiness of the house and community centre would take days to clean off, but the cold water freshened me up like a pleasant electric shock.

"Well Oliver, how was your first funeral?"

"It was okay, I suppose. No flames, no ravens, no scythes, Granny in Scotland was all right, and Fiona looked at a man."

"You saw that too."

"I've seen that man in Greater Chalfont."

"Oh?"

"Buying a paper in the paper shop."

"Oh?"

"The Daily Telegraph."

"Oh."

"Just what I thought."

"Well."

"This is nice, isn't it Mum?"

"What's nice?"

"Sharing a hotel room, just us."

"Suppose so. I mean, yes it is, like old times eh?"

"Yes."

"Do you remember going on holiday in that old camper van?"

"Yes."

"You and me against the world eh?"

"You and me and Fiona."

"Yeah."

"Are you all right Mum?"

"Yes! How's Signe, you haven't talked about her for weeks. Is she on your snapgram round robin?"

"My what?"

"Your instachat face."

"You're changing the subject and insulting my whole generation in one go. You know that, too, don't you."

"Maybe, but how is she? I genuinely want to know. I've got a very complex relationship with her. And you're all sparky, but you didn't want to leave Lancashire in the end, so I think you're still in regular, um, touch with her."

"She's okay. She's actually a bit easier to cope with at a distance really."

"No impulsive stuff possible. She never, made a pass at you or something did she?"

"A what? Sometimes I think we speak a totally different language."

"No sort of Potiphar's wife stuff, I mean."

"I do understand what you're saying there you know."

"We did read the Bible together when you were a nipper, I'm impressed you can remember."

"I'm quite impressed you read that bit out."

"I only did so on the strict understanding that you wouldn't understand it. You've broken the rules."

"Sorry, not."

"Good. Anyway, you could invite her to come down south if you wanted."

"I'm not sure I could cope with that."

"I'm not sure I could either. I think her mum might be able to."

"I think she might be able to too. We aren't very good with people are we?"

"Well I'm okay with you."

"And I'm okay with you. And you're okay with Fiona."

"And you're okay with Fiona too. I sometimes think you're better with Fiona than I am."

"But she's your girlfriend. Or wife, or whatever."

"Is Signe your girlfriend Oliver?"

"Don't be silly. She's my friend."

"God, the poor old thing. There's nothing worse than that particular eff word."

*

"Who was that man at the back with the prissy little beard you were looking at all the time and talking to in a confidential manner."

"Oh, that's Mal."

"Who's Mal?"

"We went to school together."

"I thought you hated everyone you went to school with?"

"I felt sorry for him. His parents made him wear moccasins to school. Even in the winter."

"Wow."

"He's my boss."

"Wow. You didn't introduce us."

"You were talking to Mum, and he left straight after the service. I never had a chance."

"We'll have to have him round for tea."

"You said that in a very anthropophagic voice."

"Hmm. Strange that you should both start off in Skye, and both end up in Greater Chalfont."

"I know, isn't it odd."

"I know who he is you know."

"No, I didn't know you knew. How?"

"Your mum told me about him when I came to pick up the car. Your dad had been working for him."

"Had he? I didn't know that."

"There's a lot of not knowing going on here. Does your mum know he's your boss?"

"No."

"Oh."

"And I'd rather she didn't, she's very upset at the moment."

"She doesn't like him you know."

"She never did. People just don't understand Mal."

"Except you."

"Except me.   And my dad, I suppose."

"Well, your dad did, anyway."

"Are we nearly there yet?"

"Oh Oliver you gave me the fright of my life."

"Sorry.   But are we?"

"Just coming up to Cannock."

"So we'd have been home by now."

"And have had a cup of tea and a toasted teacake."

"What are you two like?"

"Don't crow, but I'm having the time of my life in Greater Chalfont."

"There was a trace of non sarcasm in that."

"There was only a tiny trace of actual sarcasm. We're having the time of our lives in the south aren't we Oliver?"

"Yes Mum, but can you keep your voices down, I'm trying to sleep."

"Yes sir, Sergeant Major.   Sir."

*

I put my rucksack down by my bed and half jumped and half fell onto the bed.   I lay there for fifteen seconds not moving a centimetre, until I realised my neck hurt as it was unsupported and I felt hot lying there in my jumper.   The house was hot.   The house was always hot.   Mum hadn't learnt how to use the thermostat yet.   More to the point, neither had Fiona, and that used to be her job, fiddling with thermostats.   And we'd been here years.

I turned over and pushed the pillow against

the wall and got myself more comfortable. The bed creaked. It hadn't enjoyed the move down south, and creaked all the time now.

I had enjoyed the move even if the bed hadn't. It was nice to be somewhere new, to cut the strings of a lifetime and find a new path, and it was different. The people at school were different. They had their own little cliques and petty hatreds and silly things that they thought were important, but I slipped through all the gaps. I was virtually invisible. Not quite, they were perfectly civil to me, and I was perfectly civil to them. I thanked God or someone similar that I was born and raised where I was. If I'd been born ten miles further north or gone to school five miles further west I'd have been left with an accent they couldn't have failed to hold up to total ridicule. But as it was it was just about okay, if not verging on the cute for them. But the operative word was 'verging'. I was basically an accepted anomaly, and happily slipped through the cracks.

I didn't need friends because we'd moved to a house with a garden that backed onto a field that backed into deep beechwoods, and because I had Signe.

Not that I had Signe here and now or even much on the interweb as Mum still really annoyingly called it just to wind me up. I had Signe as a backup plan, an if-all-else-fails, rock solid straight up no nonsense friend who was just one step shy of being a something more. Both sides being shy, that is.

Signe had come as something of a relief. I'd found most boys tedious and shallow, and most girls haughty and superior, but even if she occasionally veered onto haughtiness, Signe was never superior, and she was not tedious and she could be deep when she wanted but she was never heavy.

I jumped up and found a biro and pulled the bed away from the wall and wrote OT♥SN on the far side of the bed frame where no-one except me could see it. The N came out a bit crap because the biro was unhappy writing on wood, but it's the thought that counts.

The sounds of Mum and Fiona talking wafted up the stairs and into my bedroom. Or Mandy, as Mum seemed to be trying to get me to call her. I couldn't see why. Some vital component of her never ending quest for parity, probably.

The voices were slightly raised, but that was all right. They weren't shouting, and in any case some shouting might clear the air a bit. Fiona was in a state, and Mum was feeling guilty because she wasn't in a state and thought she should be. They'd work it out, they always did, in the end.

I looked out of the window into the garden and up to the sky. It was dry and peaceful. I got up and walked downstairs.

"I'm just going out."

"Are you sure Oliver?   It's been a long day."

"Exactly.   I could do with some fresh air."

"Well okay."

"I'll be back for tea."

"Don't go far.   You've got your phone haven't you?"

"And two tissues."

"Take a bottle of water."

"Mum, it's January in Buckinghamshire, it's not the Gobi desert.   I'll see you later."

"Bye."

"Bye Oliver."

*

I walked by the field, ploughed and broken now and bearing no relation to the swaying ears of wheat of the summer before. The farmer had ploughed right up the fence, and walkers hadn't re-established a path that was usable yet. I stumbled and groped my way to the gap in the fence that led into the wood, and half fell through it.

Inside, the temperature increased, and any sounds dwindled. I felt my pulse rate drop and my breaths lengthen, and I touched the barks of the trees and felt their strength, birch and beech and sycamore.

The atmosphere was thick with moisture but as I reached the familiar clearing and sat on a long-felled trunk the last worry on my mind was taking a damp bottom back into our house.

My main worry lay with the people within that house. I worried that Mum would fail to reconnect with Fiona after the loss of her father. I worried that Fiona would divert her grief into working even harder for her dodgy firm doing heaven knows what, run by that strange little man with his green eyes and no sense of doubt within them. I worried that we'd end up having to move again just when I was content, more content than I'd been for years and years. I worried about Signe and her permanent sense of movement. Would she ever feel as if she was walking into a house that she felt was also a home? I sensed, in some dim and unrealisable fashion, that it was my role in life to provide that place, that home for her. That thought amused me more than it frightened me, but it frightened me a lot, and so I looked out and lost my vision in the trunks of the trees receding before me. A soft wind caught the top branches, and I felt eyes on me. I knew that I wasn't the only person who came here, there were often cans and cigarettes that I diligently tidied away, but they were more of a problem in the summer, and very rare in winter. I tried to calm my breathing but I could tell it had increased in frequency and shallowed in intensity. I didn't dare close my eyes, and tried to think that it was Signe walking her dog in the wood and if she came across me what a surprise that would be. I counted my breaths and forced the outs to last twice as long as the ins, and then flicked my eyes to the right and met the eyes of a young muntjac fifty yards away. It twitched its ears and then walked slowly away.

Giving up on receiving an ounce of comfort from the hard backed unwieldy chair, I forced my spine against it and reflected upon the love and loves in my life. I thought of spittle-moistened handkerchiefs cleaning my face clear of macaroni cheese, and afternoon naps during my first term at school, mornings only, and the warmth of my mother's embrace and the warmth of the hot water bottle she would bring me in the depths of winter, swaddled in old dyed terry nappies that were both crisp and soft somehow at the same time. She fed and clothed and held me and readied me for the world. And my father, despairing of my oil-covered hands leaving marks all over the walls, borrowing a book from the library and working with me as we cut our hands open and he swore and finally, we balanced the derailleur gears on my bike. How gender stereotyped their roles and their love was! Hers soft and unrelenting, his rough and practical and measured out in great gobs punctuated by long gaps of seeming indifference and often impatience. And then the thrusting fingers and unreasonable demands of the newly born Justin, who sucked out love for years before ever giving any back, and who I still felt owed me, even though he had been a surrogate husband for nearly three years and far away the most reliable man I'd encountered in my life. What we shared we shared much deeper, and with far more extremes of feeling, than any friendship I could remember from school. All that had seemed to be was a prison sentence of waiting, forever waiting for the tadpole tail to shrink and the adult legs to grow. Even the love that Mr Grainger had had for art was just that, it wasn't love for me (thank God, for he was truly a warthog incarnate), and though it had rubbed off on me, I looked back on it now as just a straw to cling to in adolescence, it felt almost like a sham, a chimeric part of me, an umbilical fragment that should have dropped off long ago.

No, I came to life and to love at university, and although the legs were present some childish tadpole tail remained. I tried to think of the love I felt in my late teens and my twenties, but it was a blur of embarrassment and shame, of no through roads and oxbow lakes. I thought of Shawn and was reminded of something I'd read by Charles Shaar Murray about Led Zeppelin: "The love this man is talking about is, literally, his penis."

I thought briefly of Celia, because I had to be honest and admit some lingering of those rogue feelings of my twenties towards her. I tried to notice the feelings, acknowledge their existence, and then let them go. I could see them, but I somehow couldn't quite let them go. I couldn't even see what they were.

I loved Fiona. I loved the ease with which she oozed into our lives, into every part of our lives, and how she eased every part of our lives too, oiling every cog, re-torquing every nut, changing every filter, knowing all of those words and what they meant. Tidying the shoe rack. But she had done more than tidy the shoe rack, she had put up a mirror to me and tried to sort out my actual haircut and had sorted out my metaphorical haircut at the same time, and she was like a close fitting jumper on a cold day, she moulded in and warmed me like nothing else.

But there is one love that rests above all the others. I looked down onto Oliver's closed eyes, and the small tube in his nose, and the scrupulously laundered bedding covering him. There is no love, there has been no love before and I cannot see that there will ever be again, any love in this world that can compare to the love that a female homo sapiens feels for her baby.

*

"Has he woken up?"
   "Not yet."
   "I'll get you a cup of tea."
   "Thanks love."

*

"Here you are."
   "Thank you Fiona."
   "Oh Mandy."
   "If only I hadn't let him go out."
   "Don't."
   "If only he had some normal hobbies like playing on an Xbox for whole weekends at a time."
   "Don't."
   "If only I'd insisted he carried on with the taekwondo classes."

"Don't."

"Do you have any idea how much that uniform cost? He went to three sessions. I had to pay for the whole term."

"Just stop will you Mandy. He's okay."

"He's broken his leg."

"Which will heal. And he has a cast he can get signed and preserve and turn into some kind of ... artwork."

"Shit."

"Sorry, I didn't mean. I mean, you're not going to get funny about the nature of Art at this particular moment are you?"

"No, I'm sorry, I didn't mean that anyway. It's just, the trauma."

"Look, he'll be all right. He'll bounce back. Young bones knit together soon as look. He'll forget how he broke it. The trauma you're seeing is nothing."

"I'm not talking about his trauma, I'm talking about mine!"

"Well put it on one side and think of someone other than yourself for a change."

*

If there's anything worse than someone being wrong it's someone being right. I looked at Fiona, at her unruly hair, her puffy eyes' crowfeet, and felt properly terrible. Here I was moaning about myself with my son broken in a hospital bed and my partner, and how I just felt unbelievably and suddenly overwhelmingly irritated at the semi-skimmed meaningless of that poxy little word, had just lost her favourite parent even though he was a dangerous madman. How could I be such a self-centred idiot?

*

"How can I be such a self-centred idiot?"

"Well you've had a lot of practice anyway."

"Sorry."

"It's okay."

"He's going to be okay."

"He's going to be okay.   It's a clean break."

"A clean break."

"A clean break."

"That's what we need, a clean break."

"What do you mean?"

"I mean we need to get away."

"He's got a broken leg."

"When it mends, when the cast comes off."

"You can't just take him away."

"And you."

"But I've got my work."

"With some dodgy bloke doing God knows what. You could do with a break. We could hire a camper van and bugger off somewhere. We could do that with the cast on. Clamp him in and head for the sun."

"But I've got my work."

"You've just lost your dad, they'll let you go for a bit."

"What about yours then?"

"There's always a deal to cut at a college in the

back room."

"But, no, I don't want to go really."

"Nous verrons."

*

We saw all right. Fiona grumbled, and she had a point about her mum and leaving her all alone on Skye, but bless her Helen came right back and said we were as far off in Greater Chalfont as we were on Mars and she had peat to cut and plants to plant and had carved out quite a wee niche for herself with friends there already thank you very much. Being so much closer to her husband physically than Fiona, she'd grown somewhat further away from him in every other sense. The greatest grief wasn't in the Hebrides, it was in the Chilterns. I'd catch her in the spare room, with some old fusty book about Danish playground design in the early sixties in her hands, but her eyes adrift and full and forlorn. She was in a terrible state. And with Oliver just home in his cast, wanting to be back at school but jumping at shadows, it was something of a relief to be going to work to bang some Maslow nails into carpentry tutors' heads. But I fretted there and struggled to concentrate. What were they getting up to when I wasn't at home? I had a long chat with Graham, and in his very practical manner he scouted round and found someone who had taught teaching but was back on the front line part time and was only too pleased to cover my job for a couple of months for some extra money.

*

"Are we all ready?"

"Okay I suppose."

"What am I meant to do with this cast on?"

"Look out of the window, smell the air, have some fun."

"Not very likely."

"Oh come on you two, it'll be an adventure. Like old times."

"For you two, maybe. I can't entirely cope with less than a five hundred count on bed linen changed daily by somebody else."

"You never know Fiona, you might take to it like a duck to water. You might get through a day without putting fifteen items of clothing out for the wash by the end of it. Particularly if you're put in charge of washing it all by hand."

"That was never in the agreement."

"You're sounding like a thirteen year old."

"Well this fourteen year old wants to sound like a fourteen year old. We stopped going on camper trips because they were so horrible."

"I thought you liked them Oliver. I thought you liked the Amigo."

"Well, I did. I did, a lot to begin with I guess, but in the end what I liked the most was that you seemed to like it when I said I liked it so I did. Say I liked it I mean."

"Oh."

"Oh Mandy don't worry I'm sure it's the right thing to do."

"It's not as though it's an Amigo. These seats!

They're like armchairs. And we're all in a line again, nobody's behind. The world in front, our oyster."

"Oysters have always given me explosive diarrhoea."

"Metaphorical oysters then."

"Can't say they've done my digestive system much good either."

"I always get the willies when we leave home."

"I know Oliver. It's the uncertainty isn't it?"

"Terrible."

"Lack of a known routine."

"Lack of a known toilet."

"Lack of a known mattress."

"Lack of all of your clothes. Knowing you must have brought the wrong ones."

"Exactly. Knowing you've left the one thing you need at home. Being able to see where it is, being able to go back in time to the moment you were about to pack it when you were diverted."

"My cagoul!"

"Exactly. Where were you when you were about to pack it?"

"Walking downstairs to get it."

"What diverted you?"

"I hadn't packed my book so I went back upstairs to get it off the shelf."

"And never thought about the cagoul again. Until it chucks down for the whole trip away."

"Because I forgot it."

"Because you forgot it."

"I wish we hadn't come."

"I wish we hadn't come. I've got such a load

of work I need to do."

"I've got my GCSEs."

"Will you two pipe down. Fiona, you have no work that needs doing that your great friend Malcolm or whatever his name is can't deal with for you you go on so much about how blooming marvellous he is all the time. Oliver, you are not doing your GCSEs for ages you haven't even had your choices for them accepted yet and if I have to live through another one of those parents' evenings where they go on at great length about absolutely nothing in particular I will go truly nuts and anyway they do sell cagouls abroad. They even sell them in Chorleywood which we are just about to pass if you really want to go and buy one now if it would just calm you both down one tiny bit because we do have quite a long way to go and we are going to have a good time when we get there. Okay?"

"Mm."

"Okay?"

"MMn."

"OKAY?"

"Yes Mum."

"Yes Mandy."

*

And they did have a good time. Fiona took the wheel when we crossed the Channel and relaxing suited me and being busy suited her and Oliver's temple uncreased slightly. We made gentle progress southwards and even though less than half the campsites we approached were open those that were were so happy to have some customers we were welcomed with open arms.

*

"This is the life."

"It is.   Look at those stars, you can't see stars like that at home."

"Can you see the Milky Way?"

"No."

"Look.   Right across there."

"What?"

"The Milky Way."

"No."

"It is."

"Is it?"

"Yes."

"It can't be."

"It is."

"It is Mum.   I'm the one who's meant to be a cynical teenager, not you."

"Oh.   At least you haven't needed that cagoul yet.   Even though what your friends would say with you wearing that cardigan of mine doesn't bear thinking about."

"It is cold."

"Chilly.   But nice."

"No flies!"

"Oh those flies."

"You don't know anything about flies till you've grown up in Scotland.   Nothing."

"She's got a point."

"Did you like growing up in Scotland Fiona?"

"Well I only grew up there, I didn't grown up anywhere else, so I've nothing to compare it with. It was a bit like this in a way. Except you could never see the Milky Way because it rained all the time."

"I bet that's not true."

"Or the wind blew your telescope over."

"I bet that's not true either."

"Well maybe, but you can't deny me the flies."

"Okay, you can have the flies."

"How did you like growing up in Lancashire then Oliver?"

"It's okay I sup Oh did you see that?"

"Wow I've never seen a shooting star that big."

"Where? Where?"

"Oh it's gone now Mandy it was over there."

"So I not only miss the Milky Way I miss the shooting star too. I always miss the shooting stars."

*

I may have missed the shooting star but I didn't miss much else. We carried on driving south through France in a leisurely fashion, never travelling too far in a day but never stopping more than two nights and often just one. It felt leisurely but we soon found ourselves on the left hand side of the Mediterranean coast facing the decision to either continue pushing south into Spain or to turn right to the Atlantic or left towards the Alps. The weather was very docile and so we pulled up by the sea.   A narrow coast road took us slightly northeast along what the satnav was indicating as a peninsula, although it might just have been a lagoon on our left, as the strip of land we were following widened out slightly, and small signs of habitation became apparent.

"We can't just wander on like this.   It'll be dark soon.   Where's the map?"

"I think I left it in the back."

"It's never there when you need it."

"I can't see there being a campsite along here."

"I don't know, the road's getter wider."

"That looks like a cabana they'll sell watermelons or something from in the summer."

"Not many there now."

"That almost looks like a quarry."

"Or an amphitheatre."

"Quarries don't usually have floodlights."

"Look, that looks like a campsite entrance."

"Shall we have a go?   Oliver, what do you think?"

"Looks a bit rundown."

"But that sign does say 'ouvert'."

"I think if you look underneath you'll find the 'fermé' that fell off in a breeze in November."

"Ha ha.   Anyway I'm tired of driving.   It'll be a break if nothing else, and we can retrieve the map and work out a better plan."

Well we couldn't find the map, and there was a toothless woman in a small cottage who woke up enough to show us a spot and take an outrageous fifteen Euros off us in exchange for a seriously rusty key on a long length of fairly rotten wood that gained entrance to a toilet block we all acknowledged as by far the worst we'd come across on the whole journey jostling against some very stiff competition.

If we couldn't find the map and the toilets were awful there was at least a good tap with fresh water, and we'd come with a can of tomatoes and a can of tuna and a bag of rice, and had the place to ourselves with the Mediterranean just there in front of us. The waves lapped up gently onto the beach we dragged our chairs down to with the gas lantern and cups of tea. It hadn't been an easy day driving, but I felt the tension coming right out of me and fall dribbling down the beach like a blessed gush of double incontinence.

"Telekinesis."

"What?"

"Telekinesis. If you can just make yourself be somewhere else and make that toilet disappear, this would be pretty ideal."

"It's not telekinesis, it's another word."

"Whatever."

"It's very quiet."

"It is Sunday."

"And cold. Who'd have thought the Mediterranean could be cold."

"'Hot dry summers, warm wet winters'."

"Who'd have thought it."

"It is quiet though."

"You'd expect cicadas."

"Wrong season."

"Oh I do like to be beside the seaside."

"Look, fishing boats."

"Wow, even I can see the fishing boats."

"It's a miracle, she can see the fishing boats."

"It is rather chilly though."

"Distinctly."

"Teleportation."

"You're right, teleportation, that's the word I was looking for. I'm busting for a pee, and that's just what I need.

*

We took it in turns to hold our noses and brave the toilet (anything to avoid the chemical toilet and all its attendant maintenance), and I don't know about the other two, but I slept like a baby lulled by the sounds of the sea and the lack of sound of absolutely anything else, and waking to that sound was incredibly blissful. The first thing I did was look down the edge of the bed and of course immediately found the map.

"Hello."

"Hello. Sleep well?"

"Like a baby."

"I can tell you've not had one then."

"Thanks for that, Mandy."

"Sorry Fiona, politesse only follows tea, you know that by now."

"To my eternal cost."

"I am sorry."

"And I'm sorry to go on. You found the map."

"I did, and it is a peninsula, but we're a long way from the end, and there's what looks like a sweet harbour or marina across the inlet."

"So we've come to a full stop."

"We have."

"Not an unpleasant one though."

"No."

"Shall we stay a few days?"

"And then work our way home?"

"I think so, do you?"

"Yes, I think so too. Are you glad you came?"

"I am. Thank you."

"You're welcome."

"Sorry if I was grumpy before we left."

"You've been pretty grumpy along a lot of the route too."

"Sorry."

"You've had good reason. I'm sure I've been grumpy too, except I've got no excuse, I'm just escaping my job and going on a jolly for a bit."

"I hope Oliver's okay."

"He's really got used to that cast, it's not stopping him doing owt."

"Would he be bored around here for a few days?"

"I don't think so."

"No. I won't."

"Hello love, sleep well?"

"Okay."

"We were just wondering about staying here for a few days and then dawdling home."

"Okay."

"Sure?"

"Okay."

"Okay. There was a supermarket in that last place, shall I go and get some stuff."

"I'll come too."
"We'll all go."

*

The sun came out and it felt mild.   The campsite was on a narrow peninsula that sheltered a small bay with an old port surrounded by blocks of holiday flats, although none of them were too tall. It teetered on the edge of tourism, but out of season looked rather forlorn and lost.   We had the Super-U virtually to ourselves and it was poorly stocked with anything you'd call fresh, but there was enough to gather food for a few days and we headed back to the campsite with some food, a firmer idea of the geography, and having received a couple of waves from local people passing in clapped out old cars.

The site hostess seemed to have grown back some teeth overnight and with a combination of our rusty French and her rusty English we established how many days' worth of stay and how many baguettes and croissants and pains au chocolats we required.   She didn't quite pinch our cheeks as she left our pitch, but you felt she wasn't far from it.   I'd never felt as welcomed as a tourist, and worried slightly about it.

Having bought all of this food we realised the last thing we wanted to do was prepare any of it to eat.   It was still quite early so we piled back into the campervan, and found our way around the bay to the little port to forage for lunch.

The port was charming, in a faded way. The centre was quite developed with expensive looking restaurants that would clearly have lots of tables outside during the summer. In winter it looked shuttered and in need of paint. Most of the restaurants were closed, but some were open, and it was far from a ghost town. There was a small marina and a ship's chandler with some frightening harpoon guns in its window. We parked in a small car park by the marina, and there was quite a smell of fish and some rusty hulks lashed up by a jetty that had seen better days but wasn't completely rotten.

The view from the marina was of our peninsula, and a small gap out to the open sea. It felt very mellow, almost cosy. We walked past a number of small shops to a restaurant that was clearly open, and I found it physically difficult to not stare in the window of the Immobilière. I hadn't felt at home somewhere so quickly for such a long time.

We sat in a window seat and ate a delightful fifteen Euro menu very slowly and with great pleasure.

"I like it here."

"I like it here too."

"There's a really good row of stone pines at the campsite."

"Bet there's lizards in the summer. I do like lizards."

"Probably killer scorpions and deadly flies too."

"I thought you said Scotland had the worst flies."

"It does, but they're not killers."

"Still, you said you liked it."

"I did. I do."

"I've got a terrible urge to look out for for sale boards."

"Buckinghamshire, and now Languedoc, Ms Thompson's wings are doing nothing but stretching."

"What is 'for sale', anyway. A vendre?"

"Yes."

"Haven't seen many."

"There's a board like that over there, but it's not à vendre. What's that, à loo-er?"

"A louer? That means to rent."

"I'm having a laugh, it's on a boat."

*

I've got no excuse, because I wasn't drinking. None of us were drinking. I still can't see how it happened, but we wandered over to the marina and looked at this boat for rent, and the next thing this little man with a black moustache was all over us and we were in the thing and sailing in it round the bay.

"C'est très jolie, ça."

"Oui monsieur, très jolie."

"Et Madame, qu'est ce que tu pense?"

"Oh, yes, oui, c'est très jolie."

"Et monsieur, qu'est ce que vouz pensez?"

"Does he mean me?"

"He does Oliver, what do you think?"

"It's a long way to take it home."

"Vous aimez les dames à grand age monsieur,

je vois.   Vouz ne pouvez pas avoir trop de femmes d'une certaine age."

"Sauce!"

"What did he say Mum?"

"Never you mind Oliver.   I think we'd better be going.   Merçi beaucoup monsieur, nous y penserons."

"A bientôt?"

"Bien sure, au revoir."

"Au revoir, mes charmantes."

*

"Well that wasn't what I was thinking we were going to be doing today."

"What a cheeky devil."

"What did he mean?"

"Nothing."

"It was a nice boat."

"I felt sick as a dog and it was as still as a millpond."

"And only I can swim."

"That's not true.   I got my Endeavour badge, and I'm sure Fiona can swim miles, backwards, with her eyes shut."

"Well, can you?"

"No."

"It's lucky we didn't sink then."

"I think you're right, it's pure luck that that old tub is floating at all."

*

We ambled back to the campsite amusingly worn out, and spent the rest of the day looking for lizards, which must all have still been waiting for summer to start, and then lazily eating and reading and not doing much at all, the gentle onshore breeze surprisingly chilly for the Mediterranean. As we settled down to sleep my lips felt decidedly chapped from the combination of the sun and wind and chill. They felt salt-scarred and burned and burned.

*

Oliver had become incredibly efficient moving around on crutches and sported rippling biceps. Fiona was happy to stay by the campervan reading a book and Oliver and I walked around the side of the peninsula so we could look at the village we'd eaten in the day before. We'd picked up enough food to last the day, and we took our time. More often than not he was waiting for me.

"Looks totally different from this side, doesn't it?"

"I prefer looking at it from the ground rather than wobbling in a little boat."

"That man was funny."

"Peculiar rather than ha-ha I'd say."

"The people round here are nice, though."

"Distinctly un-Gallic in their niceness I'd say, yes. And that's coming from a country where every shop owner says the equivalent of 'Bonjour Madame' when you enter."

We were wandering back a slightly different

way.   The peninsula was quite hilly, and we came
to a part that had been, not quarried, but dug out
down to near sea level.   It formed a natural
concert hall, almost circular, with steep sides of
light honey coloured stone about thirty feet high.
There were institutionalised metal seats laid out
in rows, their paint burnt by the sun, rusting.

"What's this for?"

"Don't know, it's almost like a theatre."

"No stage."

"The French really like their son et lumière,
maybe they project something onto the stone."

*

Fiona was fast asleep in her chair when we got
back, her book fallen onto the floor.   We
prepared lunch in absolute silence stifling giggles
as she lightly snored.   But then I caught myself
sniggering whilst seeing her there, vulnerable,
and tired, and still newly bereaved, and also
sweetly attractive, a tiny smile cast across her lips,
a small wave of dribble issuing from the corner of
her mouth, and I felt ashamed and protective and
just so glad to not be alone in this crazy world.
As I thought all of this, her eyes opened.

"Are you hungry, we've been making lunch."

"Have I been asleep, I didn't feel tired."

"We've only been here five minutes, you may
have only just nodded off."

"I've lost my place, not as though I particularly
cared.   Nobody is really getting anywhere in it."

We ate, and then all three of us were cast down with torpor. Oliver started off doing some vague revision from some books he'd brought so that we all felt less guilty about him missing some school. But he soon reported an inability to think straight and gave it up and picked up his phone for the first time in days instead. I found an incredible, large, leathery leaf that was still a deep green. It didn't look as if it should have fallen from a tree. I started to try and draw it, but the rigour required to even form an outline of it became almost stressfully effortful, so I just looked at it, and vaguely wafted it at my face, even though it wasn't warm. It was almost chilly. My lips still burned, and I felt a sweaty edge to my face and underneath my nose.

I suppose we must have eaten in the evening - something with rice? - but I felt as if the slightest action would consume an unregainably large amount of energy. The sun was setting. It seemed to be setting earlier than the evening before. The sky was clear, although I couldn't recall any sunshine during the day.

"I think I might be coming down with something. Feel really tired."

"Me too."

"I feel very tired and thundery of head."

"Can you hear cars?"

"Yeah."

"There haven't been cars before."

"Where are they?"

"On the road outside the camp."

"Where are they going?"

"Search me."

The sound of cars was low and incessant but not overbearing. They weren't driving fast, they weren't large cars, they weren't buses or lorries, they were cars, and lots of them. It went on for about twenty minutes. Cars. Lots of cars, driving down a road to nowhere. Where were they going?

"Shall we go and look?"

"No."

"Why not?"

"Because I have no energy to go and look, and because I don't like it."

"Listen, they've stopped."

They'd stopped.

"They've stopped."

"That's a relief."

"I think I might go to bed."

"I think I might join you."

"I think I'll read a bit more."

"Are you sure that's a good idea if you've got a thundery head Oliver?"

"It's fresher air out here than it is in there."

"Okay, but don't be late."

"All right."

And Fiona and I prepared for bed in our super-languid fashion, fuzzy of head and with a slight panic about driving a distance the following day.

My head barely felt the pillow before I was sleeping deeply.

*

"Mandy."

"Hgmpff."

"Mandy!"

"Geroof lep."

"Mandy!   Oliver's gone."

"What?"

"Oliver's gone."

"Where?"

"I don't know."

"God my head hurts.   What's the time?"

"Eleven thirty."

"In the day or in the night?"

"It's pitch dark."

We were getting dressed, trying to go quickly, falling all over the place. It was like cutting up watermelons with plastic cutlery in the rain.

"When did you notice?"

"Just now, a noise must've woken me."

"I don't think anything could wake me, I feel like death."

"So do I.   Come on!"

"But where?"

We rolled out of the campervan.   Fiona's phone's torch was bright if you shined it in your eyes, but useless against anything else.

"What's that noise?"

"Music."

"I preferred my description.   Let's go towards

that."

"Okay."

*

There was a noise, a drumming noise, or, rather, a percussive noise, coming from the area of the quarry. My head felt thick and cotton-wadded, painful and slow, and all of my limbs ached, but I felt as though I could function in a limited way. Before we'd gone to bed I'd not felt as though I had any manner of control. As far as I could tell I had retained my continence. I was holding Fiona's hand, and was glad of it.

We stumbled over unweeded low shrubs along the poorly maintained campsite access road. The air was on the verge of cool but clear and dry, and the stars bore down on us in the virtual darkness. There was no moon to guide us, just that sound.

"We don't even know if Oliver is there. He might have just gone to the toilet block."

"He wouldn't have gone to the toilet block."

"You're right. I'd soil a wedding dress to avoid going to that toilet block."

"Quite."

*

We came out of the campsite onto the main road that snaked along the full length of the peninsula. 'Main road' was a bit of an exaggeration, it was little more than a dirt track. A trace of light was visible from the quarry area down the road.

As we neared the quarry our pace slowed. There were other sounds, keyboards and wind instruments, a hint of bass, and the light was not uniform like a floodlight, but varied, not disco flashes, but with a sympathy to the rhythm of the sounds. As we reached the entrance to the quarry our pace slowed to a dead crawl, and we instinctively looked for some way in that was discreet.

Some straggly vine had grown over the rickety wire fence on either side of the quarry gate, and at one point it had weighed down on the rusted fence and flattened it. We stepped over the gap and walked through.

Most of the quarry was taken up by a fairly large number of cars most of which had seen better days. There was a small building near the gate and the combination of that and the cars obscured what was going on further inside. We crept forward and skirted the cars to get through to the centre of the action.

*

We settled by an old Peugeot that hadn't been cleaned in the new millennium and watched with a mixture of horror and comedy at the sight of fifty people, largely old people, watching a film being projected onto what appeared to be an enormous sheet, gently flapping in the wind and punctured and repaired at various points.

The film was clearly reaching some kind of morbid climax. The music was at a pitch of gnawing intensity, the percussion florid, and what can only have been a soprano saxophone was being noisily murdered, as a yacht sped out into the sea in a riot of speckled colour film, and the word 'fin' came into view.

Abruptly the audience burst into applause and cheering.   They all stood up and a number of the rickety old chairs fell backwards clattering to the floor.

"Can you see him?"

"It's impossible to tell with them all jumping around."

"He must be here somewhere."

"Well if they all go we can spot him and jump on him."

"Let's just wait."

"Okay."

*

It was frustrating.   Rather than pile out of the place, they remained standing, and someone shouted 'encore'.   And then they all started shouting it, and a man with a moustache but no hair pressed some buttons on a projector and the film ran back from one spool to the other and they all sat down and when it had wound right back and the end started flapping against the side of the projector he stopped it, carefully wound the film back through, and played it again.

*

The film had no title, but from the off it was clear that it came from the early seventies. Saturated colours and dodgy upper body hair were much in evidence, in intercut views of a little port and its people going about their daily business. I quickly realised that it was the little port across the peninsula, looking much then as it did now.

The music was polyrhythmic percussion overlaid with frenetic wind and overblown guitar. I could grudgingly give it some respect, when I realised I was concentrating on the film and its music and not looking out for Oliver. Glancing across to Fiona I could see she hadn't paid the flapping sheet any notice at all and was scanning the crowd for a trace of him.

"He doesn't seem to be here."

"Where can he be then?"

"He must be here."

"We'll have to wait till they go."

So we did. I leaned against the side of the car, and I could tell Fiona was as uncomfortable and achy as I felt. It seemed like we'd run a couple of marathons. I struggled to stay awake, aching and sweaty, loud noises coming from my abdomen.

The pace of the film had increased, and the music was maniacal, with an organ motif that was as cheesy as it was possible to be. The view of the village had changed from straight reportage to an animated plan view where bright colours replaced the old buildings with a vast new assortment of blocks of flats and stately villas dotted over the surrounding hills. The cartoonist then flew an imaginary plane out to sea and back again to show us the majestic and spectacularly ugly developments from the side as well as the top, while an imaginary pile driver pushed steel beams into the sea to create an almighty marina full of ocean going yachts for the rich and famous.

As a tenor saxophone brought back the initial theme of the music at a pace half of that of the animation, the cartoon dwelt on one yacht and returned to conventional film as a quartet of seventies beauties toasted their wealth, health and happiness in bubbly fluids dispensed from elongated glasses. They looked out onto the cartoon development, which looked cut out rather as if by a five year old with especially blunted scissors, the music sped up, and they put out to sea to the ending once more. The film had lasted about eight minutes.

*

They still called for more. The film was replayed three times until even the locals, their ageing desires for the lucky dollar of mass tourism dwindling, stopped calling for more. And then, in place of the clapping, there was an empty feeling, a void, a loss.

"Come on, go home."

A man, not the man who'd handled the projector but he may as well have been his twin, stood up and started speaking. There was a jeune or something here, but I missed most of it, but I caught a rosbif there and a murmur of a laugh here, but it wasn't a strong laugh, there was an air of regret, and then, appearing next to him, one on either side, were Oliver, and Celia.

I stood up and started walking forwards, but Fiona caught my arm and pulled me back and whispered in my ear.

"Don't do something you may regret later. Go and pack up the camper and drive it to the gates."

*

I half ran, half walked back to the campsite, thinking all the while, what is going on, why is Oliver there, why is Celia there, why are they there together? I was so tired, and so confused, my muscles ached, and I got into the campervan where I was, at long last, overwhelmed by abdominal cramps, and crawled to the toilet just before being overwhelmed by the strongest pulse of diarrhoea that has ever engulfed me.

"My son is in danger and all I can do is sit here spraying a toilet!"

It finished and I lay back, spent. There was nothing left in me, nothing at all, I could tell that if the light was on my lips would be porcelain white, and they burned and sweated horribly. I pulled my body up and went outside, throwing what I could back into the van, and then, on my hands and knees, was violently sick in one of the hedges.

"No, no, not now!"

My eyeballs were rolling in their sockets as I

staggered back into the campervan and started the engine. It shuddered slowly into life and we crept back up the path with the sidelights on. I drove as slowly as I could to keep the noise down, and reached the gates of the quarry a few minutes later. Falling from the driver's seat the stench of diesel coming from the van caught me off guard and I was sick again in the bushes we'd crept through, but, like dragging a great rock to the edge of a cliff, I reached Fiona who was still by the car.

"Oh Fiona."

"What took you so long?"

"I've had the shits something awful. What's happening?"

"Oh bloody hell. There's lots of talking and things. That woman seems to be British too."

"It's Celia."

"Well who's Celia?"

"I used to teach her. Well, not teach her, but she was a student at the department."

"What, that Celia,"

"the one with the pixie boots, yeah."

"Well what's she doing here?"

"She ought to be in Marseille."

"Are we going to have to rescue her too?"

"Rescue her from what?"

"I don't know."

*

I was fed up, weak, dehydrated, semi-delirious, and in desperate need of at least two days of bedrest. I told Fiona to go to the camper and get the engine started, waited till she'd gone, stood up, walked to the front of the group of people, and took Oliver by one hand and Celia by the other.

"I don't know what any of this is about, but he is my son and she is my ex-student and they're coming with me now. Thank you and bon soir."

We reached the van before anybody had any idea what had happened.

"What on earth is that smell?"

"Get going Fiona, we're in."

*

I must have passed out in the back of the camper van, because I awoke shoved into a corner, sat up and bumped my head. Someone had taken off my shoes. My mouth felt like mucking out hour at the hippopotamus stall, and I could tell my face was going to win no beauty contests that day if not week. I staggered from the van to find it beside a lake in a valley beside a graceful hill that was almost a mountain. Oliver was sitting on one of the folding chairs, wearing sunglasses, drinking orange squash from a glass with a straw. It looked like one of the jams of paradise to me.

"Where did you get that?"

"Sit down and I'll get you one."

"You are a pet."

"I know."

*

"Thank you. Are you all right?"

"Yes, I didn't get that bug as badly as you and Fiona."

"Oh God is Fiona all right?"

"I think we might need to get a new toilet."

"Oh dear."

"Yes, she's all right. It must have been that plat de fruits de mer."

"I thought we'd be all right because most of it was still moving around the bowl. Where's Fiona now?"

"She's walked to the village with Celia to get some food. They didn't want to disturb you."

"Nice of them. Are you really all right? What happened?"

"They were just showing this old film that someone had found, and they all got a bit emotional about it saying there was no-one new in the village, and then they dug me and Celia out and said that only young foreigners were willing to come and how nice it was we were there, and then you came and snatched us both."

"So we basically kidnapped Celia then?"

"I think she can see the funny side of it."

"So we haven't been driving all night trying to shake off a load of crazed locals waving pitchforks at us?"

"No."

"Where are we then?"

"A bit nearer the Pyrenees. Not far away from where we were."

"Oh."

*

"Oh, you're up then?"

"Yes, how are you?"

"A lot better, are you?"

"Yes. A bit sheepish. I'm sorry we stole you Celia."

"That's okay, makes a change."

"I thought you were in Marseille."

"Got a bit tired of the city, I wanted some space, a bit of light, less oppression."

"I hope we haven't ruined it."

"Well I'm late for my shift, but somehow I think I might get away with it."

"Let's just not do anything like that again, eh, Mandy?"

"Er, yes Fiona."

"We can't just pull people away from where they live, can we?"

"Er, no, Fiona."

"It was a bit weird Mum."

"Okay Oliver, okay."

"Do you want a croissant?"

"I think I'll stick to orange squash today, thanks."

*

Celia had her phone and found an excellent looking campsite for us further north of her village. We dropped her off with great big goodbyes and promises to meet up again and started the long journey home, with everyone restored and refreshed and ready for the future. I say everyone, but I felt washed out by the whole procedure. I felt washed out internally, and if I'm honest, my digestive tract never felt the same after it and I only need to look at something in a shell ever since to come over a bit queasy. But I felt a bit washed aside as well. Oliver's cast came off, and Fiona took up the reins at her job again, and Graham welcomed me back with open arms. I say open arms, but there was an ease with which Graham and Monica regarded each other, even though they were both allegedly happily married, and she'd only been covering my work for four weeks at most, that we didn't somehow gel like we had, and as time moved on, the lack of gel turned into a resentful gulf between us.

There was a sense that I didn't gel with anyone or anything when we got back.

*

I realised, using my glacial pace of self realisation, that I'd let myself go, that something had given way and fallen off, and something had to change. Nearly everything had to change. That spring I dug out the old bike, and found the tops of my thighs burning trying to scale the mountainous roads around our house. I arrived back from that first ride, face red with it all, covered in snot, heart pounding fit to burst, bush of hair almost touching the sides of the door, and went straight to the phone to book a hair appointment. But they were all busy, or didn't answer, so I got straight back on the bike and freewheeled down into town and went from one hairdresser to another until I found someone willing to cut it right then and there, even though I had to wait for her to finish her fag and I spent the whole time breathing in a heady cocktail of nicotine and last night's vodka as she hacked and harried my head into submission, and then made me quiver in pain as she straightened it out with burning red ceramic tongues.

"Hot date?"

"Only with destiny."

"Did you say desperate?"

"Destiny."

"Destiny's what you make of it, love."

*

I sat in Argos waiting for order three hundred and twenty six at collection point A, the first pair of hair straighteners I'd bought for decades, staring at my bike locked to the railings outside. It looked rusty. I started to look through a discarded catalogue at new bikes, and then rowing machines, and grip tension exercise things that looked like instruments of medieval torture. Which were instruments of medieval torture, and then I closed my eyes and took a deep breath and put the catalogue down, but it fell on the floor. I picked it up and it had opened onto a page of boxing and martial arts equipment: boxing gloves, punchbags, gloves that other people punched with boxing gloves which had roundels on them. I returned home and started to search for local martial arts classes.

*

"I don't think I've ever seen you with a fringe Mum."

"It's my new style."

"Lovely."

"Do you mean that?"

"Well. What do you think Fiona?"

"Lovely, if a little on the severe style."

"The thing is, you've always had straight hair, you're so lucky."

"The thing is, you've always had curly hair, you're so lucky. That smell of home perms, I can smell it now."

"You've never permed your hair."

"The discotheques of Portree had an unwritten rule that wouldn't allow entry to an unpermed female head at times in the mid eighties."

"You can't persuade me that Portree had discos in the eighties."

"Did so. Do you have discos around here Oliver."

"I don't want to know."

"I'm struggling to picture your school having end of year discos."

"It's worse than that, after GCSEs they have a prom."

*

I knuckled down. My bike got harder and harder

to ride so I showed it to Fiona and she oiled and adjusted and reset it and replaced the brakes and tyres on it and measured my inside leg and adjusted it some more and pronounced it suitable for casual road use. It rode better than it ever had before. It rode better than when I'd first got it. A lot better.

*

I still felt ungelled, washed out. If I was honest, part of it, well, a big part if I was really honest, was trying to show Graham I was at least as good as Monica and he ought to treat me better. It didn't work, and he resented me instead. Our desks faced each other, but when we'd returned in late August of the year we went to France there was a great big plant, virtually a tree, in between us. When he went out for the first of his interminable urinary peregrinations I looked at the label. 'Twisted Ficus', it said. It was not lying. That September a small war erupted between us, ideologies thrown at each other as we vied for the best results, the happiest lecturers, the largest increases in assessments. I kept my hair sharp and my defences on high, and I kept my figure lean. I framed a photo of Jess Varnish, helmeted and poised, impossible to tell if she was angry or just determined, and put it on my table. Graham glowered. We both received commendations, a result that satisfied nobody.

*

But I was starting to dig myself up, I was starting to find my feet. Oliver was starting on his GCSE courses and Fiona was working hard. We were moving forward. I felt able, for the first time in months, to stick my head slightly above the parapets.

*

From: mandy.thompson@arnoldsway.ac.uk
Sent: 16:01   10/14/15
To: celia.croft4759@wanadoo.fr
Subject: Sorry to kidnap you

Hello Celia

I just realised I haven't sent you an email for years and if you've sent me one I've left that old job and started working here in Buckinghamshire teaching teachers how to teach, part time.

Anyway I hope you weren't punished for missing that shift. It's not that long ago but it already feels like several years.

It's so nice being able to teach teachers and avoid the gritty end of the production line. I can even get a vicarious pleasure hearing about it, and the greatest part of observations is closing the door when you slip out at the end.

Best wishes

Mandy

From: celia.croft4759@wanadoo.fr
Sent: 02:58   10/15/15
To: mandy.thompson@arnoldsawy.ac.uk
Subject: I cannot believe you are

Dear Ms Thompson

You did email me last year to give me your personal email address, but as you'd forgotten then about what I'd last written to you it's no great surprise you can't remember what you wrote to me.

I just about avoided being sacked because of what you did earlier in the year, but I have now become alienated from the people here when I felt I was just becoming accepted to a small degree.   The summer season was poor and it feels like everyone has blamed me.

I found your son and your partner charming people but I would be very happy if I never heard from you ever again.

Yours sincerely

Celia Croft

Part five

"Are you all right Clifford?"

"I think so, why?"

"You've not touched those garibaldis and packet's been open three days now."

"I'm not in the mood for them."

"Something up?"

"Well yes."

"Spit it out then."

"It's Justin."

"Well?"

"He's got rosemary beetles and lily beetles."

"Oh and there I was thinking it was something serious."

"It is. It doesn't get more serious. They're fancy foreign pests. You're not meant to find fancy foreign pests in Clitheroe. Well, you might find one of them there, though that's unlikely, but not both. Not at the same time. Not in the same garden."

"Well where are you meant to find them then?"

"Fancy foreign places of course."

"There'll be someone somewhere who thinks Clitheroe is fancy and foreign."

"Dear God I hope not poor buggers."

"You mind your language."

"Well what's he meant to do?"

"If he's a man by now, pick them off, and in any other case he can always wear gloves. You can get them from the petrol station if you're feeling miserly."

"By, you've done it again Mum. The smell of diesel on the gloves will finish them and put off anyone following."

"Thank you."

"You're welcome."

"Oh Clifford I hope they don't do that posh roast chicken next time we go over there. I don't fancy it stuffed with either diesel or beetles."

"We haven't been invited for a while have we?"

"Tires me out all them kids running round."

"Still, it's even longer since we saw Mandy and Oliver."

"No news is good news I say, that was a champion idea of hers taking them abroad to give them a rest."

"That was best part of two years ago now."

"Two years? Feels like five minutes more like."

"No kids running round there any more."

"Long time since."

"Oliver's a proper gentleman now. Tall and clever."

"The effects of which on the maidenly nature of the females of Buckinghamshire is unknown."

"And his mother seems happy and content being his mother."

"She sounded positively radiant when I spoke to her the other day, and I can tell a mile off when she has any problems."

"And the fair Fiona seems to have borne her half-orphaned status with alacrity and emerged serene and at peace with herself and her station."

"And amen to that. It's so nice to be parents to two nice little families."

"Amen. And the nicest part is not having to wipe any babies' bottoms or teenagers' eyes, and knowing that they're not going to be barging in when some Lancashire lass's maidenliness is being called into question."

"Will you give over right now Clifford Thomspon!"

*

"Mum, are you any good at surds?"

"Is that one of those tiny countries that helped set off the first world war? I was never any good at that, the Red Hand Gang, all of that. James Bond the third."

"No Mum, it's maths."

"Maths? I'm not entirely sure why you're asking me when there's Fiona boiling over with maths and physics and all of that."

"That's the problem, I ask her and she boils over with it. I asked her what pi was a year ago."

"Now that was a mistake, even I can tell that."

"I know that now."

"If you'd asked me we'd have ended up with something nice for tea."

"And anyway she's not home yet and I need to do this now."

"Sorry Oliver you'll have to look it up online, or get them to teach it you properly in the first place."

"She's never home for tea these days."

"I know."

*

"Fiona are you any good at past historic endings in French?"

"What on earth is past historic?"

"Do I take that as a no then?"

"Yes. Surely Mandy is better at that kind of thing. She did all of the ordering when we were in France."

"She just goes on about how badly taught everything is and what she'd do to change it."

"All ideology and no work makes Jacqueline a very dull girl."

"Who's Jacqueline?"

"Quite."

"At least she's out on her bike at the moment."

"She's turned into a fitness fanatic, almost. Even worse, she's stayed a fitness fanatic. That kind of thing is meant to last a weekend and dwindle away."

"It's like she's never here at the weekend sometimes."

"I know."

*

"So tired."

"Same."

"'We all lead such busy lives these days'. Whenever I read that in the first two paragraphs of an article I never read any further."

"Same."

"Do you think Oliver's all right?"

"Not sure. He's working too hard."

"He is. Did you work too hard for your O levels?"

"I slaved for my Standard Grades, and then

almost gave up on my Highers."

"But still got annoyingly good results."

"I think the adverb you were looking for was deservedly, actually."

"Anyads you're right, he is working too hard. It seems like a hard school to me, tweed jackets with elbow patches, and that's just the women teachers.   Men who've had moustaches for decades."

"Quite a few women who've had moustaches for decades too."

"You're not wrong.   Very serious academia."

"Yes,   not   perhaps   Oliver's   natural environment."

"No."

"Still, he doesn't have to go into the sixth form."

"Well, not there anyway."

"I meant not anywhere."

"Oh."

*

I couldn't help myself at work. The combination of not having to face horrid little teenagers any more with a new haircut and the stinging rebuke of Celia ringing constantly in my ears, still hardly faded after all that time, had fired me into a prolonged phase of zealous attention to detail and mounting innovation. I could see the eyes rolling as I lectured tired lecturers tired of their students, tired of teaching, tired of me.

But then, one or two of them, slowly at first,

began to listen. They affected a world-weary lassitude when they were together, but particularly one on one, particularly one on one after an observation, they'd listened to what I'd said. They'd changed their lesson plans in small ways I'd suggested. They'd noticed the effect it had had. I looked for improvements first and made suggestions second. I kept back but also listened. I called in confidentially to heads of department to make departmental suggestions that supported individual lecturers. The individual lecturers noticed the changes. They asked for help. Some, God help me, thrived. I was thrilled.

*

They did have a prom, but Oliver wouldn't go to it. He spent the summer of 2017 getting under my feet and moping around. I tried to persuade him to go to it, getting as far as a day out in London which was fun when we were in the National Portrait Gallery, but torture when I pushed him into Next in Oxford Street to look at some clothes he could wear to it.

"I don't want to go. I don't have to go."

I sighed. He didn't have to go. I couldn't make him. I didn't make him. He didn't go. He stayed at home and festered, whilst Fiona and I went to work. We had made plans for holidays, but they were never quite right, they never pleased everyone, it seemed easier to stay at home.

Oliver avoided me all summer, it felt, but in reality, Oliver just 'avoided', full stop. He would spend hours on his phone, and then disappear off to the woods late in the afternoon and panic me he was going to fall off something and hurt himself again. I pleaded with him to keep me updated, and he grudgingly sent texts of 'OK' once an hour, on the hour. I started to chew my nails at ten to. By the end of the week he started it I had none left to nibble at all. The trouble was, as ever, I couldn't see the nose at the end of my face.

On the day after I went back to work to see if Graham had produced a new twisted ficus, the GCSE results were released, and Oliver had failed every one. Every single one.

*

"What are we going to do?"

"Dunno."

"What were you thinking?"

"You're not angry with me are you?"

"Angry? I don't know."

"Mum, you're not angry with me are you?"

"It's not a, oh I don't know. What shall I tell Fiona when she comes home?"

"The truth?"

"I suppose that is an option. I'm glad I had the day off. I was going to take you to the Green Man to celebrate. I think I might have to go and lie down."

"Do you want a cup of tea?"

"What are we going to do?"

"Glass of wine?"

"What are we going to do?"

"Glass of whisky?"

"What are we going to do?"

"Bottle of wine?"

"What are we going to do?"

"Bottle of whisky?"

"Let's put the kettle on.   What are we going to do?"

"Put the kettle on."

"Good idea Oliver, let's put the kettle on."

*

What are we going to do?

*

"All of them?"

"All of them.   Mrs Middleton said she'd not seen it at the school for years."

"What are we going to do?"

"That's what I said to her."

"What did she say?"

"I have no idea.   I think her mouth moved around a bit, but I didn't hear anything that came out of it.   What are we going to do?"

"Are you all right?"

"Not really."

"Is he all right?"

"He's a damned bit too all right really.   Made me a cup of tea."

"That's nice of him."

"I don't want him to be nice, I want him to have passed his GCSEs."

"But he didn't. Right, you've obviously been faffing around all day, where is he?"

"In his room on his phone."

"Right."

*

"Oliver?"

"Mmmn?"

"Can we talk?"

"Okay."

"Did you fail?"

"That's what the papers say."

"You know what I mean. Was it an error?"

"It's not what I wanted."

"That's not what I mean either. You sat the exams, you wrote words on to the paper?"

"Yes."

"Okay. Did you write your name correctly?"

"Yes."

"Good. Did you write your candidate number correctly?"

"Yes."

"Good. Did you write your centre number correctly?"

"Yes."

"Good. Did you answer the questions to the best of your ability?"

"I answered all the questions."

"That's not what I mean. I saw you revise. I

saw you plan your revision. I helped you revise. I saw you take steps and show diligence that indicated to me you had a thorough grounding in all the subjects I worked with you on. I saw nothing to indicate that applying the revision you had undertaken could result in total failure of your exams, so, I'm going to ask you a simple question for the second time: did you answer the questions to the best of your ability?"

"I answered all the questions."

*

"He did it on purpose."

"What?"

"He did it on purpose, failed. Not necessarily consciously, not necessarily pathologically, not necessarily vindictively, not necessarily as an Agressive Act. But he did it on purpose. He failed all of his exams on purpose."

"What are we going to do?"

"I really don't want to have to slap you in the face Mandy."

"Sorry Fiona. What are we going to to do?"

"Why don't we ask him what he wants to do?"

"Okay."

"I'll go and get him."

*

I picked up a photograph of Oliver on a towel on a beach, with an enormous sandcastle next to him. If I was honest, it was a photo of the sandcastle, with a spiralling perimeter wall dotted with turrets, each bearing a flag, a paper flag attached to a thin wooden stick. There was a drawbridge and a deep moat with square section sides. I'd sweated blood on that castle. I was petrified he'd knock it down. For the life of me I couldn't remember what had happened to it. I couldn't even remember where it was. He was nearly five. It was forever ago. They came into the room. They both looked so old, Fiona had developed a line between her eyes since her father had died, and Oliver, well Oliver was a man. A skinny strip of a man perhaps, but he was not a boy any more. It was hard to imagine him making sandcastles now. I sucked in my soul and made sure my mouth was closed. However old they looked, I felt a thousand years older. He'd never really liked making sandcastles anyway. I wasn't sure he'd ever actually made one himself.

"Are you all right Mum?"

"Yes love. Are you?"

"Yes."

"No."

"No."

"What do you want to do Oliver?"

"I don't know."

"I think you do."

"No."

"I think you do."

"I don't."

"I think you do."

"I met a man in the woods."

"That's really not a great way to start things

Oliver."

"No, he was working there, a tree surgeon."

"You want to be a tree surgeon?"

"Yes. No. I don't know."

"Did he offer you a job?"

"No. He did say he was busy though. There were three of them."

"I don't know why that makes me feel better, it ought to make me feel worse."

"Could I ask him?"

"What?"

"If he had a job?"

"You could do yes, Oliver."

"You wouldn't be angry with me?"

"No."

"Phew."

"But you didn't have to go and fail all your exams. You could have asked him, you could have asked me, earlier. You could have passed them and asked him."

"But I answered all the questions."

"Give me strength."

"Do you want a cup of tea?"

*

"Are you awake?"

"No."

"Good, neither am I."

"Mandy I'm so tired."

"So am I. What do you think about it all?"

"About what?"

"About Oliver."

"It's not my place to say."

"Why not?"

"He's not my son."

"He's fairly intimately linked to you I think."

"I don't think so. I mean, I love him an awful lot, but he's your child. What do you mean?"

"Well, I always ended up being lumbered with Shawn because you were all over Dan. And then that one time it produced the results we can see writhing in teenage agony not twenty feet from where we're lying."

"'That one time'? Are you telling me you'd never had sex with Shawn before?"

"I'm telling you nowt about it."

"You've always been somewhat coy about your histoire d'amour."

"And you've always been somewhat oversharing on the subject."

"When?"

"You used to go on and on about you and Dan and his peccadillos. Never stopped."

"I can't recall regaling you with a single peccadillo."

"It's etched into my memory like a bad smell. Anyway, you've known Oliver since before he was born, and I want to know what you think, because you're my lifetime partner and I value your opinion at this critical juncture."

"Oh."

"Well?"

"Well you've agreed with him that he's going to look into this job as a tree surgeon."

"But your opinion on the matter is?"

"I always back you up, you know I do, I wouldn't want to undermine you."

"You just think I should go back to coping with a twisted ficus between me and Graham and Oliver should ring the tree man up to see if he has a job?"

"No."

"What then?"

"I think you should go to sleep first. No. I think I should go to sleep first, I'm so very tired."

*

So I went back to the twisted ficus and Oliver asked the tree man if he had a job. Well, he said he'd tried to ask the tree man if he had a job when I came back from work, but he said the phone number just went straight onto an answerphone, so I told him to find a mobile number and ring that the next day, but as that was Saturday we agreed it was best to wait until Monday.

*

It wasn't an easy weekend. I rolled down the hill to my Mixed Martial Arts class relieved to be leaving behind the tensions of the house. Oliver was quivering at the thought of ringing the arboriculturalists on Monday, Fiona was silently fuming at the thought of his pursuit of anything lower than doctorate level education, and I was. I was.

I was tickled, if I was honest. I couldn't understand it, how he'd worked so hard and then

blinked at the exams, but there was a purposefulness to it that was admirable, a sticking of two fingers up at conventional modes of life that I knew I could never have achieved myself.

I tried to picture myself with no 'O' Levels, but failed. I was so unimaginative at that age, I confused a strictly mediocre ability to reproduce on paper what I saw before me as an artistic bent that was inherently laudable. I could laugh at it now, but at the time it felt so important, so self-defining. I could picture no work of art ever produced that was fit to stand next to the creation of Oliver, to come even close. People eulogise over ballet and Caravaggio and K.46 bleeding 6, and then feign indifference to the curl of a newborn baby's fingers around one of their own. Such philistines.

It would feel utterly perverse to most people, but I detected within myself a vivid pride for Oliver's action. I could feel vindication for my parenting. I came from a steadfastly academic background which he appeared to be rejecting in a wholesale manner. To succeed as a parent he had to somehow destroy me to supersede me, and this was an incredible blow for his independence.

Bless him. I felt pride, but I also felt totally destroyed.

*

The punches came easily that Saturday, the vocalisations were voiced a little over eagerly, the blocks parried more smoothly, the warm ups and cool downs dispatched even more impatiently than usual. The usual badinage was absent, there was an air of pure action devoid of all social contact. We arrived, practised kicking and punching the living shit out of each other, and then we departed. I cycled back up the hill sweating and worn, and ready for anything. I forced the bike up the hill at twice my usual pace, the thought of a long hot shower uppermost on my mind and our usual Saturday lunch of bread and cheese and fruit floating in front of me as I pedalled, slight olfactory and gustatory hallucinations pulling me home.

I opened the door to find Oliver sitting in the kitchen talking to Signe.

*

"Hello."
　"Hello."
　"Hello."
　"Where's Fiona?"
　"Working in the study?"
　"Right. Are you well Signe? Have you eaten?"
　"I'm okay Mrs Thompson."
　"Why don't we go to the pub for lunch? I'll just go and see what Fiona's up to."

*

"Just double you tee eff?"
　"I know: hasn't she grown?"
　"That's not what I meant."

"Your face."

"What are we going to do?"

"Oh do turn the record over Mandy. A, I've rung her Mum and she's all right about it. B, she didn't fail hers thank God. And C, hasn't she grown?"

"This isn't really helping Fiona."

"Unlike encouraging him to get a job sweeping up chainsaw chippings?"

"Do you want to go out for lunch?"

"That would be a relief, leave them to it."

"No, take them too."

"Take them too? I've not been a teenager for a very long time, but even I can see how cringeworthy that would be."

"You may have a point. Do you remember when my parents came to visit us in Darjeeling Street?"

"Remember it? I can feel my toes curling around and tickling my soles at the merest mention."

"Two course luncheon in the Crow's Nest on Albermarle Ave."

"With Dan and Shawn. How did we get Dan and Shawn there?"

"Doing their best right pair of Bobby Dazzlers impersonation. Why did we get Dan and Shawn there?"

"They were doing that impersonation well."

"Their performance has since been unsurpassed."

"Gravy stain sustained on Shawn's jumper."

"Dan managing to use the eff word not just

once, but twice."

"Be fair, he stood up with his flies undone, which diverted attention from the second instance."

"And my parents were not exactly people I respected or even remotely treated with respect. I couldn't happily sit with them through a meal with three friends without hoping a sink hole just swallowed me down in one fell swoop, even if those friends behaved perfectly."

"So maybe we won't take Oliver and Signe out for a pub lunch then?"

"Okay."

"I hope they're okay."

"Let's go and see."

*

They'd gone, or, in the argot of my youth, they had scarpered. I sagged somewhat, like a bear taking a bullet, and put on my walking shoes, Fiona following suit. We didn't exchange a word. I rang his mobile as we locked up the house, but it was turned off.

"Grr, turned off."

"Send him a text."

"What shall I say?"

"'R U OK?'"

"I think I prefer 'where the bloody hell are you Oliver?'"

"Each to her own."

"There, I've done both."

"They may have just gone for a walk in the

wood."

"That really isn't helping, Fiona."

*

It was a beautiful day. It was lunchtime on a beautiful day at the end of summer in the Chilterns and birds chirped in the hedgerows and fat flies drowsily hovered over cow parsley fronds sprawled across the pavement. It had rained hard in the night but was sunny now, and the earthy smell of fruiting mycelia topped a bouquet heady with the scents of a fecund summer.

*

The house we had rented was an old estate cottage, maybe a gatekeeper's cottage, and stood some way from the edge of the town. We turned into the main road leading down to civilisation, and approached a seat which was next to a bright yellow grit bin. Fiona had a set to her face that she adopts when there is a task at hand. As we set off down the hill I wished I'd just sat down on that seat. I was so tired. It wasn't the thought of going down the hill that bothered me, it was the knowledge that we'd have to come back up it at some point.

"Where do you think they went?"

"Station?"

I wished we'd come in the car. It was hardly any time since I'd been cycling up the hill.

The tree-lined road gave way to a small

residential area and then the road flattened out
into the town proper. We had been walking very
quickly and I could feel my face was very red, but
Fiona looked fresh as a daisy as ever.

"Slow down a bit."

"Oh, okay."

She took out her phone and squinted at it as
we walked along, slightly slower now but still fast
enough.

"Next train leaves the station in seven minutes,
and then the London one in ten."

"We should be able to get there."

*

We did. An attendant let us onto the platforms
and we jogged over the bridge for the westbound
train. Two teenagers were waiting for it, but they
weren't the teenagers we were interested in, and
although lots more boarded the London train,
Oliver and Signe weren't among them.

"Well that's a relief, what now?"

"Go home?"

There wasn't an answer to that. He'd turned
off his phone, he hadn't taken off on a train. I
couldn't imagine anybody eloping by bus.

We dragged our weary heels back through
town, slower but still at a fair pace. I could feel a
slight click in my left hip with every step, and both
of my femoral tendons ached to their very cores.

"My femoral tendons ache to their cores."

She wasn't listening. We were in the busiest
part of town at its busiest time of the week.

Normal people doing normal things, not plagued by runaway exam failing sons and their floosies. I was vaguely annoyed by having to avoid all of these lucky people, and was struggling with a strong desire to throw them into the road, when Fiona grabbed me by the arm.

"Wait!"

She pulled me to the side of the pavement and we looked into the window of a clothes shop. I could never work out how it paid its rent. The stock was awful, dated stuff with overworked collars and thick synthetic fabrics in gruesome shades. I'd never seen anybody go in it.

"I don't think this is the time to be shopping for clothes Fiona. And if it was, I don't think this is the place."

"Wait. Now glance round into next door, table by the counter. Carefully."

We swapped places and I peered around the edge of the clothes shop into the window of the shop next door. It was a café, a busy café. And sitting on a seat in front of the cash register, next to each other facing out, were Oliver and Signe.

"It's Oliver and Signe!"

"You don't have to whisper."

"What are they doing?"

"I'd say, and I'm no Sherlock Holmes, but, they're having lunch. Just like we should be. I don't know about you but I'm starving."

I looked around again.

"I could swear they're having soup."

"Come on, let's go home."

*

We walked up the hill much more slowly than when we came down. As we neared the top, we started to slow even further. I glanced over to Fiona. She wasn't the focused and determined person she'd been on the way down. As we reached the seat next to the grit bin she made a funny sound and sat down.

"Come on Fiona we're almost home."

"I cannot walk one more step."

"You look a bit peaky are you okay?"

"I feel drained and weak, I feel like I might slur my speech, my arms feel worse than my legs. My legs feel awful."

"You sound a bit hypoglycaemic."

"Oh my God. I don't want to be hyperglycaemic, I want to be weak, a bit pale, a little full of nineteenth century ennui. I'm not a medical textbook glossed over at the age of eighteen, I just can't walk home without a bit of a rest."

"You can be as melancholic as you like if you want, I only asked."

"I'm just worn out and I haven't had my lunch, that's all."

"And it's hypo-, and not hyper-glycaemic."

"It's doing my head in, that's what it is."

"Irritability is another sign of it, too."

"I don't want 'signs' and I don't want 'symptoms', and forever being shown differentiation between the two. Can't we be normal? Oliver cut his hand the other week and it swelled up a bit, except it couldn't swell up, could it? Oh no. It had to have oedema, didn't it."

"I thought you liked precision in things."

She opened her mouth to say something and then closed it again. Like a landed fish, I thought nastily, and caught myself before I said it.

"Let's get you home and sitting down."

"I don't want to sit down."

"And irrationality is the most conclusive sign."

She growled. I lifted her arm. I knew she'd be happier at home. She didn't resist, but her arm felt heavy, and her head bowed down, and we didn't move with any speed, but I finally got her back and put her in the sofa and poured her a pint glass of barley water and got out a bag of rice to microwave.

"I'll microwave some rice and chop some things into it, won't take two minutes. Well, maybe three."

I heard her grunt, and knew then that things would be all right. As I reached up to the microwave I saw a note attached to it.

GONE TO GET LUNCH

COULDN'T BE ARSED

TO WAIT FOR YOU

BACK IN AN HOUR

OLIVER X (AND SIGNE)

I sighed and put the bag of rice in. How had

I missed it?   Why on earth had they put the blasted thing there?

*

"Better?"

"Yes.   Sorry."

"It's all right.   I'm sorry, dragging you off like that when you needed your lunch.   Did you have a snack mid morning?"

"No."

"You know you're much better when you have some nuts or something half way through the morning.   Honestly, I leave the house to do my karate and you flake out and Oliver brings in immigrants."

"I was about to have some nuts when he asked me if I could pick her up at the station."

"Lazy little gets."

*

What can you do?   There was nothing to do but wait.   I put the small amount of dishes the microwaved rice and chopped up bits had generated into the dishwasher and took Fiona a banana and forced her to eat it, and she made me eat an apple and then we sat next to each other on the sofa and the next thing I knew I was aware of Fiona pulling away from me and the house was noisy enough to indicate that Oliver and Signe were home again.   I felt warm and soporific, stood slowly up, kissed Fiona on the forehead and went out into the kitchen thinking beautiful thoughts. Everything was going to be all right. Her hair smelled right, so nothing could be wrong.

*

"Hello kids, let's get that kettle on and have a cup of tea."

"Oh, um, actually Mum can you take us to the station? I'm going to go and live with Signe."

*

"My baby!"

"It's all right, she's all right, he's all right, her mum's all right, they're not too far away."

"Thetford!"

"It's not far away."

"And her mum is not all right. She's a nasty piece of work, a cutter down of people."

"Well she's going to have to accommodate a hopeful cutter down of trees."

"And I bet there aren't any trees near Thetford any way."

"Mandy there are trees every where there are people, getting in the way of people and needing to be cut down."

"He loves his trees he won't be able to do it."

"He will."

"And the danger, the saws, the climbing, the falling down of tons and tons of wood."

"Oh come on."

"The splinters in his fingers!"

"I can't see him getting within reach of a saw for a very long time and I'm sure those kinds of places are boringly obsessed with safety. I can see him raking up leaves and twigs for at least three years. It's probably good for the soul."

"If he can even find a job."

"If she's anything like the nasty piece of work you say she is she'll have him a job before you can say knife."

*

She did. I calmed down. He'd gone. It wasn't what I'd planned. But I hadn't planned anything, I just hadn't envisaged him doing anything other than going to university. And he was happy. I hadn't realised he wasn't. I don't know how I hadn't.

*

Dazed by the whole thing, I settled back into my battle with Graham, but if I was honest, my heart wasn't in it. My heart was broken slightly, my heart was in Suffolk, or Norfolk, or wherever Thetford was. I pined for it, and in the October half term we went to see him. To see them. They were in a house like ours, an old estate cottage. Except ours really was a cottage, but theirs was a cottage only by name, more like a residence for His Lordship's favourite mistress within short riding distance of the Main House. It had a minstrel gallery, and I imagine the rent was at least double that of ours. It shared that hollowed cheek feel though, the waiting space before moving out to an ideal property. We were given a room with twin beds. No home has a room with twin beds in, unless it has twins in it.

*

"I miss Lancashire."

"That's just what I thought."

"Did you?"

"Or do I mean, I miss a home of our own?"

"That, I think."

"Sorry."

"I don't blame you, that house was tiny."

"Tiny, but it was ours. Yours, anyway."

"'What's mine is yours'. Ours."

"Euch. At least I didn't say that to you about my debts."

"But it is ours Fiona. We could always sell it if you want to move to Buckinghamshire. I'm enjoying living there more than I thought."

"You are aren't you. You've got the bit between your teeth."

"It's quite nice being a foreigner, sometimes feels more welcoming than being at home."

"I'm not sure about that, but if I was honest, I preferred being a foreigner in Lancashire than being a foreigner in Buckinghamshire."

"You weren't working as many hours there, that's for certain."

"I want to reduce them. We're always on the verge of an easy life, and some problem crops up."

"Holding the baby.   Can't you tell him to lay off?"

"We're just so close a breakthrough, it'll revolutionise submarine data packet transfer, but splitting the signal to obviate disruptio"

"That sounded like she was banging a gong for luncheon.   This place!"

*

I was a trifle uneasy about facing Paula Nilsson again.   The woman had accepted my resignation and was now accommodating my son under her roof.   She had a distinctive nose and brutal eyebrows, and was offensively slim without actually being thin, but she had learned one lesson well which was how to treat people, and in her line of work that was unusual as well as being lethal.   She'd be able to get a cobra into any basket you liked without the use of a single musical instrument.

"Arnolds Way, eh, Mandy?   Do you like it?"

"It's all right.   A bit small."

"Solid Two all day long.   John muddles along, but he muddles along well.   Still, he was absolutely legless at the last meeting."

"You're joking."

"Nobody else noticed.   He downed a couple of bottles at the meal.   It was very nice wine, he wasn't alone, but Butters from Hartlepool had three and stole the limelight."

"What are you like."

"When you get us together we're awful, is the

only honest answer. I'd not got John down as a drinker though, he's a bit of a slow burner. Chews his food well. Probably soaked it up a bit."

"I thought you all had exemplary characters."

"When the mice are away, the cats will play."

"Charming. So you collect skeletons in a little black book do you?"

"You never know when you're going to have to call in a favour. It's human nature."

"You never stay anywhere long enough to let any mud stick I suppose."

"She always grinds the skeletons into bonemeal and sells it to the horticulture department."

"Signe, darling, you know I'd never sell a bone to an agriculture department that I could have sold to dog owners through animal care at twice the price."

"I said horticulture."

"You're mistaking me for someone who actually gives a toss."

"Yes well your prospective son in law might give a toss about the distinction, given that that's what he's doing."

"That's very funny darling, because I was under the impression that Oliver was enrolled on a forestry course."

"It mainly seems to be a health and safety course."

"I jolly well hope so Oliver, I do not want you coming back home at Christmas without an ear or several digits, or having lopped someone else's off."

"What about you Fiona, do you teach art too?"

"No."

"Well I suppose Mandy teaches teaching now, don't you."

"And the thing is, teachers don't want to learn about teaching just as much as students don't want to learn about anything from the teachers who can't be bothered to learn how to teach."

"On the sea shore. So what part of the teaching game are you in then, Fiona?"

"I'm not, I mean I don't."

"Really? A civilian. Rarely spotted in these parts."

"Oh, I was under the impression that you were just in charge."

"Touché."

"No, I mean"

"It's all right Fiona, you've found her Achilles heel, that's all."

"But what I meant"

"You see Fiona, in the dim and distant past I did teach, and quite enjoyed it, God only knows I may be deluded but I think I was actually quite good at it sometimes, I still get a Christmas card from one student"

"Note the 'one student', and that's when the Post Office manage to catch up with us on the never ending roadshow of college calamities and"

"That's quite enough now Signe, we've been through this so many times."

"It's lovely salmon."

"Thank you Oliver."

"Bet it's M and S."

"Signe!"

"Sorry, I know you'd never stoop so low. Charlie Bigham of course."

*

"I hope it's not always like last night Oliver."

"Of course not Mum, Signe's usually much nicer than that."

"I wasn't particularly referring to Signe."

"And you were just about okay."

"Very kind."

"Now make sure you give Fiona plenty of notice where to stop, this is a fast road."

"Just up here, about another hundred metres. ... There, pull up over there."

"Those hedges?"

"Yes. Well, Glen did the tops, but I did all the sides."

"They're very straight."

"Course I was mainly sweeping up the clippings."

"What is it, privet?"

"No, elaeagnus. Ebbingei, I think."

"Oh."

"And Mum, what you said about Christmas. Paula has asked me to stay and meet her husband when he comes back from New York, and I said okay. I hope that's okay."

"Oh. Okay."

*

We had arranged to meet Paula and Signe at the pub for lunch. They were taking Askia for a walk together. Paula's car wasn't in the car park when we arrived, and nobody was going to volunteer to sit in the pub and wait for them.

"I'm starting to get nervous, it's ten past now. Has Signe sent you a text Ol?"

"No. They're not usually late."

"Really?"

"Well, not much anyway."

"What part of the waiting game are you involved with then, Paula?"

"Come on Fiona, you can't blame her for thinking you're some kind of teacher."

"Christ, I don't look like one do I?"

"What do you mean? Do I?"

"Well, yes."

"What do you mean? I don't wear corduroy. I've never worn corduroy. Do I look like a teacher Oliver?"

"Do you want an honest answer?"

"Of course not."

"You look nothing like a teacher Mum."

"Thank you. I think you're going to have text her you know."

"They'll just be a minute, I'm sure."

"Are you all right?"

"I just don't like a fuss, that's all."

"Do they do this all the time?"

"No."

"You've gone rather red."

"Look, here they are."

"At last."

"Don't say anything Mum.   Please."

*

"Two beef, one turkey, one pork, and one vegan cutlet please."

"Any extras?"

"Yorkshires all round please, okay?"

"Err."

"Well, one vegan Yorkshire then please."

"I'm afraid they're not available as vegan Madam."

"I'll have a large Glenfiddich then instead please."

"Certainly.   Thank you."

"Thank you."

"Since when were you vegan Fiona?"

"I'm not, I just fancied something different."

"But no Yorkshire?"

"I'm just not that into them.   Oh, thank you. Good health."

"Cheers.   I'm so sorry I overlooked you yesterday evening."

"That's all right, my favourite flight is always under the radar."

"Like your work?"

"How do you know about my work?   What do you know about my work?"

"Nothing in either case, I just surmised."

"Hmm, well you surmised wrong then."

"How was your dog walk?"

"Just the usual one Oliver around the Grange's boundary.   Was your hedge still there?"

"Yes, look Signe can we play pool."
"Sure."

*

"Are you sure you're okay about all of this Paula? I mean he's not being a pain in the neck is he?"

"Mandy he's absolutely saved my relationship with Signe. He's so reasonable, and perceptive, and honest, and I can tell you she is the opposite of all of those things. Well, she is with me anyway. She's sweetness and light with him of course."

"And he's not holding her back on her A levels or anything?"

"They sit on either side of the dining table and do their homework at the same time. I'd never say it with them here but it's very sweet."

"So he's doing some book work?"

"Arbortop have told him in no uncertain terms that they'll only keep him on if he gets five GCSEs by the end of the year studied in his own time."

"Wow. He didn't tell me that."

"He didn't tell me either, I just have closer contacts with his tutors than you might imagine."

"They'll be petrified about the whole thing."

"They had a three on their SAR and they know I'm on them anyway. Hort is always a mess. Everyone is on their toes, but that's far better than being on their dignity."

"What's Signe going to do?"

"Go to Oxford to do PPE, conversion course to law, star pupillage, director of international NGO before thirty (title to be specified) and then Prime Minister before forty."

"Oh."

"That was the last thing she wrote in her diary she thinks she's hidden anyway."

"Oh."

"When's that food coming? That dog makes me starving every time. It's about time it did the decent thing and keeled over it's already three years overdue."

"They're coming back."

"I wish they'd get better at pool. I was always top at pool at university, weren't you?"

"Don't remember playing it much."

"What about you Fiona, what's your physical exercise poison?"

"I've always found that the contemplation of Newton's fourth law burned off all of the necessary joules, actually."

*

Fiona and I drove back to Greater Chalfont mostly in silence. Even as the M25 dragged to a halt by South Mimms, the main noise was the swish of the windscreen wipers.

It was dark when we arrived back, and the dank atmosphere outside followed us into the unheated house. There was a slight smell I hadn't noticed before, but that didn't mean it was new. I closed the curtains.

"Do you want your mum to come here for Christmas?"

"I'm not sure I'd want to inflict this place on her."

"It's all right."

"It's all right, but it's nothing more, and it's a long way for her to come."

"We could go there if you want."

"I'm not sure she could cope. I don't think you could. I know I couldn't."

"No."

"It was nice here last year, the three of us."

"Yes."

"What about going to your parents'?"

"Well they always go to Justin's."

"Or we could invite them here."

"I'm starting to understand your inflicting thing now you've put the boot on the other foot."

"We could go away, go abroad."

"What if Oliver had a wobbly, I want to be here."

"Yeah."

"Shit."

"Well, I don't think we need to worry about Signe being overwhelmed by it all and generally exploited."

"Not immediately, no."

"I mean, some of it was funny."

"Yes. Are you all right Fiona?"

"I'm just tired."

"Same."

"Work tomorrow."

"Great."

"Fancy a wee dram?"

"I fancy a big whopper one."

"That's my girl."

*

As usual I was up first in the morning, clanging and clanking around the kitchen, clearing up left messes, boiling kettles and toasting bread, rubbing eyes and turning on lights. The house rattled in its de bas en haut, minimalist, ready to be folded up and put back on to the market in a couple of hours manner. Paula's house had had a parquet floor through all of the historically non-servant areas. Ours had cheap laminate covering what was probably heavily stained linoleum. They both rattled though. There were no ink-splodge pictures and accumulated ropey old oven gloves to soak up the sound. I wondered if any of Signe's ink-splodge pictures had ever been attached to a wall.

"Penny for them?"

"I'm not jealous of Paula."

"If I was her husband I'd be finding a reason to stay in New York."

"This place is getting on my nerves. Do you want to move down here?"

"Not really. Do you think we'll need to open a new jar of marmalade?"

"Definitely."

*

That Monday started poorly. An email from the agents in Lancashire saying that the tenants in our cottage were complaining that someone had knocked on the door, twice, asking for me. What could I do about that?   (The only silver lining from this was the thought of somebody asking for me. I didn't think there was anyone left there who cared about me at all.)   Graham playing his petty power games again - I was certain he'd moved my desk about ten centimetres towards the wall again. He denied it, but then got shirty when I moved it back, or, as he put it, 'moved it forward onto my side'.

I had an observation from ten thirty to eleven thirty, and getting out of the office came as some kind of relief.   My student was Giles, a business studies lecturer who was fairly new in post.   He had responded well to the lessons in the last year, but he was so out of his comfort zone his pips squeaked.   We had a chat before his class came back from their break.   He was already sweaty, and my first note when they filed in was to tell him not to wipe his hands on the sides of his shirt as it made the material translucent and you could just about make out the moles on his torso.

The group was surprisingly compliant for a teacher with such a low level of confidence.   They were learning about Gross Domestic Product, but my eyes were drawn out of the window to the quadrangle of the college, and a spindly cherry tree in the middle.   I thought of Oliver and his course which seemed much more interesting than this.   He had been rhapsodising about the new equipment he was learning to use, the chain guard, kickback zone, oiling, chaps, helmets, gloves.

I pulled myself back to the lecture, the bored but polite children, teenagers, students, young adults. Had they failed all their GCSEs and ended up on this nonsense course? He'd moved on to a video with an animation about means of GDP calculation and intercontinental comparison methodology. It seemed as far removed from Buckinghamshire as was physically possible. I looked back at the cherry tree. The students had pulled chunks off it, but it still had some leaves near the top. Or the crown, as Oliver had told me to call it.

Giles was getting the class to split into groups to debate the validity of GDP as an indicator of the economic health of a country. They were designing posters and rehearsing arguments, and before I knew it it was time for me to go. I gave Giles an encouraging smile, and steeled myself for Graham's icy glare on my return to the office.

*

I couldn't wait to leave the college and go home, but when I got there it was empty and cold and I had a fat head. I had no energy to go out on my bike or engage in vigorous exercise, so I sat down with a cup of tea and read the paper.

 30/10/2017   06:16PM

 Fiona mob2

Going on here, won't be back till

seven thirty sorry. F x

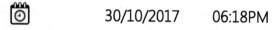

30/10/2017   06:18PM

Fiona mob2

Sorry to hear spag bol ok? ILY Mandy.

30/10/2017   06:27PM

Olly Mop Mob

Hello Oliver hope you've had a good
day there's a tree at our college needs
your magic touch thinking of you lots
Love Mum

30/10/2017   06:32PM

Fiona mob2

I've got a sandwich here you eat
without me I'm starving! F x

I sat on the sofa, eating a microwaved bag of rice
with bits cut up into it, listening to Richter

hammering out Pictures at an Exhibition. I could hear a fox outside, but inside the piano pushed the staleness of the air away from me for a while, and I put down my plate and surrendered myself to Russian winters past.

*

"Coo-eee!"

"Blurm hello Fiona. You look suspiciously perky. That's not fair on a Monday evening."

"Got a lot done, shouldn't be late tomorrow. I'll make us a proper tea for once."

"That'll be nice. We used to have proper teas all the time"

"when Oliver was here. I know. So we need to have them again, and we will, and we must. You must be parched, your mouth was lolling wide open, do you want a beer?"

"I don't know."

"It's not illegal. Yet."

"We could go to the pub!"

"Steady tiger, you may have had a delicious half hour snooze, but I have just come in from a hard day at work, and now that I am home, I do not want to be kept long from my bed."

"Okay missus."

*

30/10/2017   10:14PM

Olly Mop mob

I do love you mum but off my case!
O x

*

I dragged my lumpen body, weary from a poor night punctuated by the curdling screams of the fox and vivid by tantalisingly unreachable half memories of dreams of bad school days running down corridors to escape. Escape what? Escape who?

Graham. He'd definitely moved my desk today.

"I'm going to have make marks on the floor now."

"Marks can get moved, you know."

"We used to get on Graham. I gave you a yoghurt once. You put your hand on my shoulder when I'd had a bad day and a: it didn't feel creepy, it felt like support, and b: I really don't normally like anybody putting their hand on my shoulder and I would be really sensitive to it being creepy, so it must have been support."

"That explanation went on a bit didn't it?"

"Are you saying me explaining it was creepy in itself then?"

"No. Actually I'm touched."

"Oh."

"Sorry Mandy, I knew I'd crossed the mark when I started moving your desk away."

"Well when did you start?"

"Last week."

"I didn't notice."

"I moved the plant at the same time so it was less obvious."

"You devious little bugger."

"The thing is, it's not thriving, I was worried."

"So you blamed it on me, like you've blamed everything on me since the departure of the fair Monica."

"Sorry."

"So are we all right again?"

"Okay."

"How can you sulk so long?"

"Oh, very easily, I haven't really spoken to Dom since he gave me a three on a visit in 2012."

"But he's your boss."

"Win-win situation really."

"You are terrible."

"Thanks."

"Why don't we move the thing nearer the window anyway. It probably needs more light."

"Probably be best to just chuck the stupid thing straight out of the window."

"You can't do that, it's a living thing."

"I have this aversion to living things."

"I had noticed."

"Shucks, you're all compliments this morning aren't you Ms Thompson?"

*

I got home early, but not to the usual empty house.

"That's the first time you've beaten me home since forever."

"Mmmmn?"

"Are you all right?"

"Not really."

"I didn't think so. Do you normally chop onions that fine?"

"Onions?"

"Yes, those white things at the end of your hands, next to the scary sharp knife you've no idea about either."

"Mmmmnn?"

"Shall I cook tea?"

"Pizza please."

"I think we should start with the knife going down actually Fiona."

"Okay."

"That's good. Now come through here and sit down. I'll put the telly on for you while I cook. Eggheads, you like that don't you?"

"Mmmn?"

"I'm taking that as a yes. I'll bring your water through for you."

*

"Sorry Mandy, I think I must have been miles away."

"Bit further than that I think. Are you better now?"

"Yes, you see it works, it finally works, and instead of making everything easier, it makes everything harder."

"I thought you'd be coming home earlier when it was finished, whatever 'it' is."

"I probably ought to be worried whether I've got a job at all."

"But he's your old friend, and he offered you a job. Didn't he?"

"I only had a contract to complete this work. It should've been finished ages ago, he might well find me very poor value for money."

"We've still not had him round for tea."

"He's really not a round to tea kind of person. And I've hardly seen him recently anyway, he's out trying to sell what we've done."

"Well what will be will be, I think I've learned that harder in the past few months than I ever have. We can manage. I'm sure there's still a Conservative club around here I can work behind the bar in. You'll never guess what, I only made up with Graham today."

"That's something then, and this is really lovely. I'm sorry if I'm distracted."

"It's all right, are you sure work is the only thing bugging you?"

"Yes, well I keep on getting these funny emails."

"God it's ages since I've had a funny email trying to sell me Viagra or lengthen my penis. They're from so long ago, you almost miss them somehow."

"These aren't like that."

"What are they then?"

"Sort of trying to sell me something, wanting to know what I want, asking really random questions like which sports I like, how much I spend on clothes every month, if I prefer citrus fruits or apples and pears."

"No, I haven't seen those, whenever I pass Graham's computer there's an advert on the screen for a sweet Chinese lady you'll love to meet, if she's not Russian. They're just building up slow to that."

"The thing is, I keep reporting them as spam, but they come back with another name."

"Just so long as you don't click on a link you should be all right."

"Well that's it, there's no link to click."

"It'll give up soon I'm sure. Shall we just stay here for Christmas, you and me?"

"Why not, but can we go to bed now please?"

*

"Graham?"

"Yes Mandy."

"Do you ever get emails asking you funny questions, like how many pairs of socks you have, or if you prefer sprouts to parsnips."

"No thank you very much. Who could answer that anyway?"

"What?"

"Sprouts or parsnips?"

*

It was a long week. I experienced a semi out of body experience when I was observing an electrical installation lecture with glacial pace and a cracked sense of invention that mixed the words current and currant in a manner that was neither clever, nor amusing, nor useful in any way. I wondered how the teacher maintained any semblance of control, but then realised that the students were in an even worse state than I was and we were minutes away from needing an ambulance.

"Were that alright like then?"

"I think we've got quite a lot of work to do here Dean."

*

I had to force myself into karate that Saturday, and my lacklustre kicks and punches, my dismal vocal ejaculations, were treated with scorn by my fellow trainees, and I cycled slowly back up the hill, my tail between my legs, my knees splayed slightly, the pedals rotating fitfully.

I lumbered into the house, the empty house, and rolled onto the sofa, and wondered where Fiona was.

There was a sheet of paper on the dining table. A half sheet. A sheet folded in half. Its presence annoyed me, and I forced myself up to retrieve it.

Hope you had good karate

Had to go to meeting with Malcolm back

late afternoon

Don't do too much!

F x

"That's no good for me mate."

She'd ripped the piece of paper out of the printer, and the biro she'd written the note with was still on the table. I picked up the unread newspaper and took all three items back to the sofa and spent the following hour drawing Fiona.

I drew her as Mary Shelley, lying on her back in a small rowing boat floating on a lake, but the hair was all wrong. The boat was okay, but the mountains were awful. Her nose was crooked.

I read the paper, or at least moved my eyes across some of the texts and pictures, more over the pictures than the texts, but none of them to an extent that I could have answered questions on any of the subjects.

I tried the crossword. Gibberish. I tried the quick crossword. For a year at school we'd done the Guardian's quick crossword every wet break time, 'we' being me and two geeky friends. We'd always got it done except for between one and three clues. There had been a lot of wet break times. I couldn't even remember their names, and I couldn't answer more than three clues today.

I put the paper down and fell asleep.

*

"Hello."
"Hello."
"Have you been back long?"
"Quarter of an hour?   Something like that."
"You didn't wake me."
"No."
"Did you sell the thing?"
"No."
"Shall we go out for tea?"
"Not really bothered."
"You look tired."
"Mmmm."

*

It wasn't an easy autumn.   I was pleased to be getting on with Graham.   I was making progress with most of my students.   Some of them were doing really well.   A couple were at the point where someone should be talking to them about alternative careers.   The twisted ficus was thriving in its new position nearer the window. We'd started calling the IT leader Snake Hips Simone, and it was passably amusing.

Oliver was calling home once a week on a Wednesday evening.   He was enjoying his course; he was enjoying the food Paula provided; he was enjoying his work more than his course; he was getting on well with Signe and she was doing well on her A level course.   I hated every last minute of it.

Fiona was still working for Malcolm, but I could tell it wasn't easy.   She'd become evasive, and found the television a useful tool for avoiding eye contact. If I asked any questions about her work she batted them off or pretended she hadn't heard, and then got ratty if I repeated them and didn't answer them at all. She started coming home a little bit later every day, to the point where we started eating separately most of the time.

*

As Christmas loomed ever larger on the horizon I started to panic at the thought of not only having to think of presents for Oliver without being able to casually slip oblique questions into mealtime conversations, but also having to find presents for both Signe and Paula, and even possibly for Paula's husband. I could hardly not do so, given that they were accommodating my son under their roof and had refused to take a penny for the pleasure of doing so. I had to buy them presents, and they really had to be good ones too.
      "Do you know when you'll be home tonight?"
      "Not sure, things are hotting up a bit."
      "See, he can't let you go."
      "No, seems he can't."

*

In line with standard Departmental practice and normal modes of reasonable behaviour, Graham and I were spending the ends of most afternoons Christmas shopping online and bitching about the worst student teachers. On good days, we spent the beginnings of the afternoons like that too.

"I literally felt like I was going to die."

"Look, a hand carved soapstone ball that's a puzzle and a tactile objet d'art."

"Too late now, it'll be held up at customs. Anyway, it's probably made by some poor prisoner who's paid a pittance if that."

"Like everything else isn't?"

"Genuine old penny from their years of birth turned into a key ring, that's my parents sorted. Fully ethical, completely personal, doesn't take up space, what's more to like?"

"The key ring part will have been made by your prisoner."

"You won't let go will you."

"Are you having your parents round?"

"Not after what happened to the Christmas tree a couple of years back. No, we're off to Barbados."

"Lucky thing."

"Probably spend more time in Heathrow but it's the thought that counts. It's her idea of course. I think I'd rather be in the Chilterns, wrapped up by the fire."

*

After all of that stress Oliver sent me a list, I ordered it all online, it arrived, and I posted it special delivery on the nineteenth, then spent the week at home, bouncing off the walls, trudging through slush to buy things we didn't need to entertain people who weren't coming, and putting in some work on the admin for letting out our house in Lancashire.

Christmas Eve was on a Sunday, an odd day for it, and Fiona worked right up to the twenty-third. She came home from work on that Saturday in a terrible state, just at the point my dad would have been settling down to listen to the final scores to work out his pools, and it struck me, because Fiona seemed to have forgotten all about football, and it had once meant so much to her.

"You look awful, you should be happy, last day at work, feet up, nobody to impress, light up our fags and stick a ready meal in the oven. Heaven."

"He wants me in tomorrow."

"You what? He can't, it's Christmas Eve. It's Sunday. He can't."

"He wants me in tomorrow."

"He can't. It's against the law."

"He wants me in tomorrow."

"Who else is going in? I mean, who is being forced in?"

"He wan"

"I said, who else?"

"No-one else."

"So why you?"

"Mandy."

"Why you?"

"It's been getting rather hectic."

"What way hectic?"

"Hectic hectic."

"Has he assaulted you?"

"No."

"Don't look away. Has he done something

Not Quite Right?"

"No. Oh."

"Do you fancy him?"

"Shit."

"Answer the question."

"No."

"Does he fancy you?"

"How can anyone know that."

"I think you do know.   Does he fancy you?"

"No.   I don't think so."

"Are you sure?"

"Yes, pretty much."

"One hundred per cent?"

"Pshaw."

"But you don't fancy him?"

"I've always admired him.   He built a rocket in top juniors that burned a shepherd's shelter down."

"That's not a comfortable mental image."

"I'll be all right."

"If you were going to be all right you wouldn't have come home in such a state."

*

I rang Oliver up that evening without sending him a text first and he wasn't happy.   He was fractious and grumpy and complained that Paula had had to go and pick the parcel up at the Post Office and they hadn't given it to her because it was addressed to Oliver and not her and she didn't have his ID, so they'd had to go again together and it was a forty minute wait to get it.   There was a terrible din going on in the background and I asked him what it was and he said Nils was home. When I came off the phone I tried to make a joke about Nils Nilsson but Fiona wasn't into even trying to be amused that evening. She left for work early on the Sunday and promised to be back before noon.

*

I made a point of having a lie-in, which translated into lying in bed, developing a headache, when I'd have been far better off getting up and getting on with something useful and practical like peeling potatoes. So I got up and cycled six miles through damp streets spattering my clothes with mud that I took a very small amount of pleasure in washing. All of which strenuous activities took me to eleven thirty. The barren house mocked me. There was a gnawing feeling in my empty abdomen but I felt the least hungry I had ever felt in my life. I felt the least Christmas-y I had ever felt on a Christmas eve, even worse than the Christmases I'd boycotted in my late teens and early twenties out of a feeling of revolutionary zeal. The reality was I'd resented the reduction in presents which had dwindled to the point that Mum was getting far more than me just from her friends at her knitting club.

Knitting! I made a cup of tea, and moved my eyes across sheets of the paper, and resigned myself to the fact that knitting was not only on the horizon, but was sailing towards me at speed. If not literal knitting, metaphorical knitting.   I thought of great aunt Nellie and her year long preparations for the Sale of Work.

I threw the paper down.   It was twelve o'clock and I couldn't care less which novels were the best of 2017 and what the latest accoutrement was for a North London Christmas dining table.   I wanted my Fiona, and I wanted my Oliver.

I was all alone on a wet and cold Christmas eve. I wanted my mummy.

Part six

"Who was that?"

"Mandy."

"Oh. Owt up?"

"Not that I could tell. You know how she goes on."

"Aye she does that, she can't help it though, she's"

"Since when have you been such a male chauvinistic pig Clifford Thompson?"

"I was going to say, it runs on my side of the family."

"Were you heck as like."

"Before I was cruelly interrupted. Anyway, what was she going on about?"

"Oh I can't remember now, Fiona was late or something, and she's still moping about Oliver leaving home."

"Child leaving home in this day and age at that age sounds like as near to a miracle as you can get. You hear about them bouncing back till they're in their forties."

"Doesn't seem right."

"You can say that again, some of the shenanigans we got up to in our digs on my apprenticeship the lads at home were green to their gills I tell you."

"Not that and that really doesn't sound right. No, I mean Oliver leaving, it's not right."

"He's doing what he wants, I've never heard of anything more right."

"Trees want cutting down all over the country, he should be with his mother, there were trees all over the place when we went down to see them all."

"Oh let's not go back there in a hurry love, that train journey and all of those people in London. There's enough people in Manchester let alone all them lot."

"The trouble is you've no ambition Clifford. You used to want to see the world. You used to get up to your shenanigans, as an apprentice and for a short spell after you met me too."

"That impure mind of yours was the first thing that attracted me to you."

"Give over. Still, he seems happy, living with a Principal too, what a coming up in the world for a Thompson that is."

"She's just jealous of us going round Justin's for Christmas tomorrow."

"If she'd actually been there last time we were she might not feel so bad."

"Now don't start over those potatoes again."

"It wasn't just the potatoes. Where, I say, where, was the pudding?"

"She just comes from a different place that's all."

"I've tried to imagine a place that doesn't serve Christmas pudding but it's got me stumped."

"Anyway, I'm sure she's just nervous, and Fiona'll be home soon, and Oliver'll be with them for the New Year, and isn't it about time that girl just calmed down and looked forward to life rather than worrying what it's going to do to her."

"I'll drink to that."

"Aye. Shall I crack open that Sherry so we can?"

"What a good idea. Trouble is she's led a charmed life but she just won't see it."

*

"Are you all right? You look like you're going to cry, or laugh. Are you all right?"

"Both. Yes, I am. Oh Mandy, he proposed!"

"You what?"

"So much for living in communes and wearing sandals all year, he proposed, as in normal marriage, the evil stain on a civilised society, rings on fingers and names written down in the Illuminati's black ledger."

"Well?"

"Well what?"

"Did you accept?"

"I told him to stick his ring, up his ring, and suggested a manufacturer of bearings who might make them swivel together in a smooth manner."

"Oh well done Fiona, so what did he say?"

"He sacked me."

"Oh thank God for that."

"I told him the only person I'd ever consider marrying is you."

"That's sweet."

"Well?"

"Well what?"

"Will you?"

"What?"

"Marry me you stupid woman!"

"If you want."

"But do you?"

"I rather like it as we are. We Are, you know."

"I know. Love you."

"Love you."

"What have you had for lunch?"

"Cup of tea."

"That is a fatal mistake, let's crack open that bottle of Bailey's, I don't know why you bought it."

"For just such an occasion."

"Who's that at the door?"

*

"Oliver! Signe!"

"Hello Mum, hello Fiona."

"What? Why? How?"

"We're here. Signe blew a fuse with her mum and dad going hammer and tongs at each other. We've been on lots of trains. Is it okay?"

"You could have called."

"And ruined the surprise? We brought a Christmas cake, and your presents, and our presents."

"Are you all right Signe?"

"I'm never going back there."

"I'd better ring your mum and say you're here."

"I'll do it."

"Thank you Fiona. I think I need a sit down. What are we going to eat?"

"What have you got?"

"We were going to have a curry. Makes a change."

"Curry and Christmas cake. What more do you need."

"Another bottle of Bailey's might help."

*

The doorbell rang again. Feeling massively shaken, I yanked open the door.
"Hello Mandy."
"Hello Shawn."